A PORTION OF
THE LOVELINESS

CHRISTOPH FELDKIRCHEN

Feldkirchen Press
ISBN-13: 978-0692716434
ISBN-10: 0692716432

Cover by Jupp Majchzah
Front cover photograph by the author

This is a work of fiction.
Any similarities to any persons living or dead
are purely coincidental.

TABLE OF CONTENTS

NOTHING COULD HAPPEN

Once, I remember, we came upon a man-of-war anchored off the coast. There wasn't even a shed there, and she was shelling the bush... In the empty immensity of earth, sky, and water, there she was, incomprehensible, firing into a continent. Pop, would go one of the six-inch guns, a small flame would dart and vanish, a little white smoke would disappear, a tiny projectile would give a feeble screech – and nothing happened. Nothing could happen. There was a touch of insanity in the proceeding, a sense of lugubrious drollery in the sight; and it was not dissipated by somebody on board assuring me earnestly there was a camp of natives – he called them enemies! – hidden out of sight somewhere.

-- Heart of Darkness

One

In boot camp there is always scuttlebutt. It floats from company to company, and you hear it around the concrete laundry tables while you scrub and pound your wash to death, or in those rare moments when you can sit in the barracks courtyard to smoke and relax. There was this Missouri farm kid, see, over in Company Thirty-seven. He'd never been away from home and he sure missed his ma and pa and most nights he cried himself to sleep. His Company Commander called him "Okie" and his fellow boots kidded him because he wasn't too swift. Anyway, last night he crawled out of bed and made a rope from his sheets and blanket and a couple of shirts. He tied one end to his bunk and the other end around his neck and jumped out the window, but the dumb fucker made the rope too long and broke both his ankles when he hit the asphalt two stories down.

And what about that street-gang Mexican from L.A., the one who used to be in Company Twenty-four? He punched his Company Commander, a first class petty officer. They say he was really goaded into it, but now you can see him, a rifle balanced across his forearms and a bucket hanging from it, double timing with a guard, moving a pile of sand from one side of the base to the other like a human egg timer. All day. It's sort of the same way you break a mean horse.

Then there are, of course, the main topics of conversation. Great Lays I Have Known, How a Broad's Mind Really Works, and What I'm Going to Do to the Bitch When I Get Home. And guffaw stuff, such as the story of the boot discovered making it with a sock. Get it? Or a tale of envy, about the guy who crawled over the fence three nights in a row without being caught, to drink beer in a motel room and make

3

it with his girlfriend, who had driven all the way down from Pocatello.

Once you accepted the fact that your life was the Navy's and no longer your own, boot camp wasn't all that bad. You marched, and ate, and smoked, and performed endless menial tasks. You went to lectures. You had a toy gun that you kept clean. It was easier than the Army or Marines but tougher, they said, than the Air Force. A Marine boot is taught to kill, but a Navy boot is only taught to obey orders without thought or hesitation.

When I entered boot camp in September 1965, I wasn't in very good shape. I had been drinking and smoking too much, and ate and slept irregularly. That first morning they rousted us out at five a.m., and we shuffled in a rough formation to the mess hall. Then we stood in line and waited. I fainted, and was allowed to sit on the curb with my head between my knees.

After breakfast the ritual began. We had our hair cut, and were left with about 1/16th of an inch all over. We were given underwear and socks, a jacket, work shirts, pants, a little blue recruit cap, and a brown canvas sea bag in which to put them all. We were fitted for shoes and measured for dress uniforms. We spent the afternoon with stencils and paint, indelibly marking every item with our name and service number.

The next morning we gathered all the belongings we had brought from the outside world and marched to the post office. Except for shaving gear, all our toiletries were confiscated. We were allowed to keep cigarettes, lighters, combs, wallets, watches, and bibles. Everything else had to be shipped home. They frisked us to make sure we weren't holding on to anything.

We had inoculations, and dental exams, and intelligence and aptitude tests. We were fingerprinted. We stood inspection. We learned to make a tight bed, stow our gear exactly, wash our clothes by hand, and march in formation.

Our Company Commander was a chief petty officer, a boilerman. I was later to understand what that must mean in terms of long hours spent in the hot airless guts of a ship. He was older and probably gentler than most of the men pushing boots. His surname, which I suspect he sometimes regretted, was Little. He was a small man, with neat white hair, striking blue eyes, and glasses with clear plastic rims. He wore a large diamond in a heavy gold ring, and would whack you in the head with it if you looked around any while marching. "Quit'cher gawkin!" he would say.

We went to church on Sundays. The sermon was usually inspired by the Old Testament, usually involved battle, and always stressed the strict religious duty of absolute obedience. Jesus, we also learned, was no coward or quitter. Those who wished them were given pocket-sized New Testaments. I still have mine. The flyleaf reads as follows:

> This New Testament is presented by your
> Chaplain and comes from the American Bible
> Society acting as the agent of the churches
> of America. It is an emblem of the continuing
> concern of your church for your moral and spiritual
> well-being while you serve with the Defense Forces
> of our Nation.

You were never alone. You were roused before dawn, you showered and shaved, made your bunk in the only prescribed fashion, smoked a quick cigarette in the courtyard if you had time, and marched to chow. Each day had some highlight: a shot, a lecture on military justice, a film on drunk driving, a swimming test. That test, supposedly in order to keep the pool clean, was preceded by a shower in which you had to soap all over, then rinse thoroughly, then bend over and have your asshole inspected to make sure there were no soapsuds left there. I assumed it was just another way they had of making you feel like a thing. I wondered if they thought it was a way

5

of checking for signs of homosexual activity. I wondered if the two lifeguards doing the inspecting enjoyed their work.

To pass the swimming test, you had to jump off a low diving board, swim a circle around some floats, and climb out of the pool. You couldn't just say "I can't swim." You had to show them. If you wouldn't jump off the diving board, they took a long pole with a padded end and pushed you off. If it looked like you were drowning, one of the lifeguards jumped in and rescued you, and you were signed up for swimming lessons.

After the swimming test, we went to chow and then mustered at attention by our bunks for announcements and mail call. "Listen up, you pukes," the Chief said. "I got the results here of the GCT smart test. I'm gonna post 'em, but I thought y'all might like to know that Feldkirchen here made a perfect score, a seventy-five. Y'all can't get no higher than that, and it's a damn sight more than most of you squirrels made. What ya think now, Feldkirchen, you think you're better than the rest of us?"

It took me a moment to answer, and all I could think to say was "Not better, Sir, just different." Better, different, it didn't really matter, now that the cat was out of the bag.

I was not, in fact, a typical recruit. I was scholarly, mild-mannered, twenty-two years old. Most other recruits were eighteen. I had been to college on and off for five years, and had even studied in France for six months. After France, I lived more and more in what might graciously be called a state of existential confusion, compounded by the Cuban Missile Crisis and the assassination of JFK. I was finally asked by the school to leave.

I didn't go far, however. I was working as a photocopy machine operator in the college library when the notice arrived ordering me to a pre-induction physical. I passed it easily, and didn't know what to do. Steeped in nineteenth century traditions of romanticism and revolution, I considered myself a socialist, perhaps an anarchist, maybe a poet. I knew the Cold War was a plot to keep people frightened and dutiful, and that organized religion was a sham. As for Vietnam, it was obvious that the U.S. was involved in a murderous, misguided attempt to prop up a series of oppressive and corrupt regimes. I assumed that if I were drafted, I would probably be one of those hunnerd thousand Muricans that LBJ had just announced he was sending into the jungle. I didn't want to kill, or be killed. A few years later, when there were hundreds of thousands of draft resisters, it might have been easier. But by then it was too late for me.

I quit my job and decided to flee to Canada. Since I had loved France, I drove three thousand miles from Palo Alto to Montreal. I couldn't understand the patois, rented a depressing hotel room for two dollars a night, and wandered the streets for a few days, eating in wino cafeterias and thinking about looking for a job. Then, in a fit of loneliness, I drove back to Northern California.

There, I decided to apply for conscientious objector status. I sent away for the forms, and received them with a letter saying that if they weren't returned in ten days, I would automatically be drafted. In 1965, guidelines for objection were strict. To qualify, you more or less had to be a Mennonite or a Quaker, or have a long background of religious activities demonstrating your sincere pacifism. The way they had worded the forms, I could not fill them out. The fact that I was, like Shelley, "a nerve, o'er which creeps the else unfelt oppressions of the earth," would mean less than nothing to them. I never was much on self-esteem or strength of character, and no longer had the will to beat the system, or the courage to defy it. My life was about to become a cliché; I could see the writing on the wall. The sea, however, could save me from the jungle. The U. S. Navy could be my safe harbor.

The Naval Reserve Center in San Jose was a large quonset hut with a back yard full of jeeps and trucks and little gray cannons on wheels. I took a written test and a physical.

7

I was presented to an officer who administered the oath. I swore to uphold and defend the Constitution of the United States, and to be governed by military justice. I signed a piece of paper. The officer congratulated me, and I drove home to Palo Alto.

It seemed the height of irony. I had grown up in Long Beach, a Navy town, and had always thought swabbies slightly ridiculous. We would laugh at their funny round hats and the way they swaggered down the street with their wallets stuck in their waists. Once a year or so a drunk one would stand up during the roller coaster ride at the Pike and either fall to his death or smash his head against a beam at forty miles an hour. When I was ten or eleven, a bench on American Avenue where I would wait to catch the bus was right across the street from a jewelry store. Different women would stand in the doorway and make a sales pitch to the sailors who walked by. Many of the swabbies seemed quite interested and went inside, and I eventually figured out that those ladies were probably offering more for sale than rings or watches.

Now here I was, signed up for two years of active duty. If I were lucky, I might be assigned to a ship in the Atlantic or Mediterranean, or wind up typing in an office in San Francisco or Seattle. At least I would never have to pull a trigger, and probably wouldn't see Vietnam at all.

That evening, I had supper at the apartment of a woman I worked with at the library, and much, I think, to the surprise of us both, I ended up spending the night with her. A week or so later I went down to San Diego to report for boot camp.

I reported to the wrong gate, and they had to send someone over for me in a pickup. Recruits were coming in large numbers in those months, and it only took a day for a full company to be formed up. I had determined to stay as invisible as possible.

I wrote letters when I could, to various friends and to Miranda, a woman of beauty, intelligence and humor, with whom I was hopelessly and unrequitedly in love. I also wrote to Mary, the woman I had been with the night I enlisted.

Miranda responded with short, marvelous notes. Mary wrote long, chatty gushers. Most of my other friends didn't know what to say, to a sailor.

In some ways, boot camp was good for me. I ate and slept well, and gained weight. I had plenty of exercise, and no booze. I developed a sort of hodge-podge spirituality. In the previous year or so, I had been reading more and more about mysticism. This had been sparked by Colin Wilson's *The Outsider*, a book which entered my life accidentally and with the force of a bombshell. I then read his *Religion and the Rebel*, and branched out to Alan Watts, Huxley, D. T. Suzuki, and the 14th Century English Mystics. It was mostly, at that time, an intellectual exercise. The closest I had come to a mystical experience involved late afternoon sunbeams filtered through a cumulus haze of red wine, codeine, and infected wisdom teeth.

I began to practice what I thought of as a sort of Zen awareness. Each menial task I performed, such as sweeping a barracks or cleaning my toy rifle, I tried to do with full attention and detachment. It made it easier to go through the day, and even provided a sort of high. I would also look long at the few natural objects in view: a cloud, an occasional tree. But it was far from true meditation, and it left me when times turned rough.

One day our company boarded a bus and actually went off the base, driving out to a firing range somewhere east of San Diego. It felt to me like heaven to be riding along a street, looking at the shops and people. At the range, we were given real rifles, and I had to pull a trigger after all, but at least it was only to shoot at paper targets. We also had a fire-fighting session, and had to crawl on our knees through a burning building. We had two classes in tying knots, a skill I still haven't acquired, and spent some time on a landlocked plywood ship. We learned port from starboard, bow from stern, and how to salute the flag when coming aboard or going ashore.

We continued to practice marching, and became better and better. One morning we were on the parade ground in a dense fog. You couldn't see ten feet in front of you. Nothing existed but us and the sound of the recruit captain's voice. He was a burly Polish kid from Pennsylvania, and that morning his commands were sharply timed and right on. We were moving as one organism, and we all knew it, and it felt very good.

I caught a chill that morning, though, and it grew worse. The Chief wouldn't let me report to sick call until I was so ill I could hardly walk. I checked in with a good case of bronchitis. That night in the base hospital I was burning up with fever. If I lay on my stomach in my bed I could look out the window, across a short space of lawn and through a high chain link fence at a street full of traffic. Across that street was freedom. There was even a bar I could see. As sick as I was, I wondered if I could make it over the fence for a drink. Problem was, they had taken away my clothes.

My temperature was becoming higher. I looked at that chain link fence and remembered one from the summer when I was six years old and my brother and I were enrolled in military school because my mom had gone back to work. They made us play softball without gloves, and afterwards your hands would be red and tingling with pain. When my team was up to bat, I could stand with my fingers hooked through the chain links and watch the cars go by on the street and wish I were home.

I had never encountered sadism in adults before. During lunch, at a certain time they came up behind you and filled your milk glass with water, no matter how much milk was left in it. And then they made you drink it. Mine was usually about one-third full of milk, and I would forget that they were going to sneak up behind me, and the result was a watery chalky fluid that looked disgusting and made me feel like throwing up, and a couple of times when they made me drink it I began to cry.

The man in charge of my age group was named Sarge. He always wore a khaki uniform and one of those little peaked campaign hats. Sarge didn't think much of me, especially after the day we were in the gym and he decided we would have boxing matches. He sent me over to the office, which seemed miles away, to get some boxing gloves. I came back with only one pair, and he made fun of me and sent a bigger kid down for a second pair, and then made the two of us box the first match, and he actually seemed to enjoy seeing me get beat up.

He had a favorite game during play time. He would take off his belt and hide it in the gym, usually somewhere under the bleachers. Whichever kid found the belt could run around whipping anyone who hadn't managed to make it out the door. Then the finder would hide it again in the gym and the game would continue. Sarge encouraged kids to hit really hard with the belt and always stood by the door to push the cowards back into the middle of the room.

The belt rose and fell on the backs of the children, and the young men were running through the streets with the bulls close behind them. Hemingway stood at the door of the gym letting the brave ones pass through to safety. In Arles, after the bullfight, they hung the bull up by its hind legs and we watched the butcher cut it in pieces to be given to the orphanage. Four of us had driven down to Provence for the weekend, and Randy and Dan and I had no end of fun pulling Rawlins' leg. He wanted to be so sophisticated and kept forgetting the word *afficionado* and asking us to pronounce it until finally we told him *afinkionado* and drilled it into his head and he actually told the English girl at the café that he was one, and she laughed at him and the poor bugger didn't know why. He also believed us when we told him the Roman amphitheater at Orange had been in perfect shape until the Nazis bombed it. Rawlins became an Air Force officer after he graduated, and I had hoped they hadn't put him in charge of anything. But here we are, Rawlins is flying the plane, and the rest of us are scared bootless. "Our mission is to bomb

11

Hanoi," he shouts back from the cockpit. "We're going to set Hitler back a thousand years. Wait just a minute though, men, I'm going to stop in here and see if they have a copy of *Life International*." He banks to the left and we go into a tailspin and are headed straight for the café where the English girl looks up just before everything turns into a ball of flame and boy is she no longer laughing. The ball of flame glows cozily in the fireplace of the elegant eighteenth-century drawing room. A man and woman are seated near me in ornate chairs. Their features are delicate, drawn, and wasted. Her skirt spreads wide around her, touching the floor. Her bodice is low; the tops of her breasts bulge forth as if we are in a Hollywood movie. She is brushing her long brown hair. The man gazes into the fire, his hands idly holding a small volume of Aeschylus. Another man, exquisitely dressed, paces back and forth in front of the hearth. He has a slight limp, and a smirk on his godlike face. I realize then who they are.

"Ethereal, other worldly," Byron says to me, "and all these other things they call us. It's humbug, you know. Look at us! Shelley leaves a trail of abandoned women behind like little dog turds. He and Mary beget squalid brats who quickly die of neglect. I have travelled half the globe, sheathing my sword in any orifice I could. When Shelley's body washes ashore, it will be green and bloated and one-third eaten by fish. At the cremation there on the beach, after Trelawny plucks Shelley's heart from the fire, I will puke in the bushes, then traipse off like an idiot to save Greece and die of an absurd fever. Mary will return to England and a long career as a prick-teasing bitch. So just leave us out of it, sailor, and go back to sleep."

Three or four days later, I was well enough to return to my company. It hurt to smoke, but I wasn't about to give it up. We had a session with the personnel men about our future. Many of the four year enlistees would go on to a school and become radio operators, electricians, mechanics, etc. It seemed like all the African-Americans were designated as

12

boilermen or enginemen, so they could be confined below decks. As for the two year enlistees, we were just warm bodies and wouldn't be around long enough to deserve much. This was an angle I hadn't figured. I didn't look forward to mopping, sweeping, chipping, and painting for the rest of my hitch.

Our orders arrived a few days before graduation. I was assigned to a destroyer stationed in San Diego. A Destroyer! When the graduation ceremonies were over, most of the company were proud to be in dress blues with seaman apprentice stripes, and to wear the little round white sailor hat. They strutted and preened and could hardly wait to be home walking down Main Street. I looked at myself in the mirror and felt ludicrous. The first thing I did when released, carrying my heavy duffle bag, was to drink enough scotch so I could stand to be seen in public. Then I rode a bus up to Long Beach, where at my parents' house I had some civilian clothes.

Two

In mid-November, I reported to my ship in San Diego. She was the USS Buckett, and I'll leave it to you to imagine what her nickname was throughout the fleet. Before going aboard, I stood on the pier and looked at her. She seemed a jumble of gun barrels, torpedo tubes, smokestacks, dish antennas, radar screens, and countless other menacing structures, but she was newly painted and appeared almost sleek. She was fairly new, built in the late fifties down in Pascagoula, Mississippi. She was four hundred feet long and forty-five feet at her widest point. Her innards were crammed full of engines, boilers, mechanical devices, computers, storerooms, and ammo magazines, but somehow there was still space for about 15 officers and 250 enlisted men.

I was processed in and given a temporary bunk. I fully expected to become a deck ape. As it happened, however, the ship's Weapons Yeoman was ending his enlistment, and I was assigned to replace him. Yeoman is the Navy term for a clerk; thus, I did the routine clerical work for the Weapons Department and its officers. The department consisted of the Deck Division, Gunnery, Fire Control (i.e. the radar and computers that aimed the guns), and Anti-submarine Warfare.

Though I was only a lowly seaman apprentice, the job conferred certain privileges. I had a small office, deep in the bowels of the ship, its ceiling criss-crossed with pipes and cables, its walls lined with instruction manuals marked *Confidential*. It was just large enough for two desks and a safe. The second desk was for the Weapons Officer, but he was hardly ever there, as he preferred to work in his stateroom. That office, as cramped and depressing as it was, helped keep

14

me sane over the next year. Most sailors are never alone. They live and work in crowded, confined spaces over long periods of time, and the toll on their nerves is inevitable. I had my private retreat, my own monkish cell. My duties were not all that onerous. Typing, filing, running errands aboard ship or to the base, updating reference manuals and trying to ignore the fact that those manuals all pertained to devices designed to kill people.

One of the first things I learned after reporting aboard was that right after Christmas the ship was headed for the Western Pacific (WESTPAC) and Vietnam.

I was assigned to Second Division, with the gunner's mates. They were a mixed lot of older petty officers and green young strikers. Most were closed-minded, prejudiced, and profane. Some were sadistic; a few were obviously unstable. Many had one or more tattoos. There were snakes and panthers and bleeding hearts with knives through them and the names of women or ships. The most colorful gunner had tattooed above his penis the words "Danger, Swinging Boom."

The sorriest personality was Murchison. He was a second class petty officer who shortly after I arrived on board ship was promoted to first. It was his harsh growl that we heard every morning after reveille sounded over the loudspeaker. He walked around the compartment, sticking his sallow face down close to those of us who still slumbered. "Rehvulley, Rehvulley, get'cher ass outa the rack!"

He was a big man, with curly graying hair, sad eyes, and a face scarred by smallpox or acne. He had broad, stooped shoulders and a slight paunch. He had a key ring on his belt with about a hundred keys. Everywhere he went he was accompanied by a small gray cloud of gloom that expanded or contracted according to his mood. A loner, he was not part of the buddy buddy crowd of the other gunner's mates. Twice he had left the Navy to try and make it on the outside, but twice he had returned. Later, in WESTPAC, a story from home spread through the Weapons Department. The day the

Buckett left port, some of the wives got to drinking, and Murchison's old lady called up the base Operations Office.

"Has the Buckett gone yet?"

"Yes Ma'am, she has."

"You sure she's gone? She ain't broke down again or come back or anything?"

"No ma'am, she's at sea all right."

"Then tell me something, honey. How big a cock you got?"

The most likeable gunner was Josephs, a third class petty officer. He had a genuinely honest, affectionate nature, and he didn't judge people. He had been a second class petty officer, but had been busted for going on sprees. One evening after chow, he came up to me as I was dressing to leave the ship.

"I seen you reading the other day," he said. "What d'you read, shit kickers or fuck books? Me, I read both."

I groped around for an answer. This was a simple literary classification they hadn't learned about yet in Freshman English. "I mostly read novels," I said.

"Do they have lots of fucking in them?"

"Some of them."

"I tried reading one of them once," he said, "but it had too much talking and not enough fucking." He drifted away. I assume he had been hoping to trade with me for something he hadn't read yet.

I went ashore and took the bus to my locker club. I changed into civilian clothes and had three or four scotches in the quiet, darkened bar of the U.S. Grant Hotel, then went to a movie, had a few more drinks, changed back into my uniform, and returned to the ship. This was my normal pattern, except that when there was no movie worth seeing, I just drank.

I usually had a slight hangover when Second Division mustered on the fantail every morning at seven thirty. One morning in early December, before we were to spend two days training at sea, I was called aside by Mr. Hooper, the Division Officer.

"Feldkirchen," he asked, "do you have a general quarters station yet?"

"I don't think so, Sir."

"Right," he said, looking at a list he held in his hand. "Then I'm assigning you as a first loader on Mount 32." He walked away, and I looked up above the quarterdeck to the 02 deck, where Mount 32 was. Its twin barrels, each about ten feet long, were carefully covered in clean white canvas.

When you enter or leave port, the special sea and anchor detail is set. My assignment for this was as a lookout on the flying bridge, the open area on the roof of the bridge. That mid-December day was the first time I had ever been to sea in anything larger than a motor boat. Within a few hours I was seasick and had lost the entire contents of my stomach.

By mid-afternoon we had reached the training area. General quarters sounded and all hands reported to their battle stations. There were eleven of us assigned to the mount. Two others were also sick, and we had a pail nearby in case we needed it. Josephs was the mount captain. He lectured us in how the gun worked, and what our separate duties were. As one of the four first loaders, I was to stand up next to a gun barrel and keep my side of the firing chamber filled with ammunition. We were going to fire at little rafts adorned with large yellow flags. The rafts were pulled through the water on a thousand-foot cable by tugboats.

I wasn't sure that I could bring myself to put the shells in the gun. It wasn't what I had had in mind. Being on a destroyer wasn't what I had had in mind either. Being in the Navy at all, in fact, wasn't what I had once envisaged. I didn't believe in this war, remember?

The big gun up forward began firing at the raft. It missed, and you could see from the splash where the shell had landed about thirty yards beyond. The second and third rounds missed also, but the fourth blew the raft into several pieces and left the flag lying on the water like an overturned sail.

I wondered what would happen if I simply refused to put the shells in the chamber. I had this mental picture of Josephs yelling at me and maybe hitting me, and then the Gunnery Officer coming down and giving me a direct order and my refusing again and being led off and locked in a compartment somewhere and winding up in a brig, carrying sand or busting rocks and getting kicked around, for what? My scruples would be thrown in my face, my punishment wouldn't stop the war, and some other poor slob of a seaman would be up there on the mount stuffing in the shells.

I stumbled over to the pail and puked again, some long dry heaves that brought nothing up because nothing was there. I stood with my hand against the bulkhead and looked at the gun. Every bolt and seam stood out gray and distinct. The sky behind was an artificial, Technicolor blue. Josephs was a cartoon Popeye preparing the gun for action. The canvas covers came off the barrels. The mount was rotated from port to starboard and back to port again. The barrels were raised and lowered three or four times, and then Josephs pushed the button to check the firing mechanisms. Nothing happened. He tried a few more times, then tinkered around with this and that, and then reported up to the bridge that Mount 32 was down and unable to fire. He still didn't have it fixed by the time we docked in San Diego the next evening.

I was in Long Beach for Christmas, and left my civilian clothes there, as we had been told enlisted men could not take them to WESTPAC. We were to visit Hawaii, Japan, Hong Kong, Taiwan, and the Philippines. I had gathered a small collection of good books and stored them in my office safe. I assumed I would have plenty of time to read at sea. I was a nervous wreck.

Two days before our scheduled departure, problems were discovered with the ship's boilers. The departure was delayed. There were rumors of faulty maintenance, perhaps even sabotage by someone who didn't want to leave San Diego. The

Engineering Officer was relieved of his duties and transferred off the ship. It probably wasn't his fault, but someone always has to take the blame in cases like this.

It was not clear how long the repairs would take. The delay only gave me more time to brood. I had made no friends on board ship, nor did I want any. None of them seemed to realize what they were doing. The officers were all arrogant blockheads, and from the Captain to the lowliest seaman apprentice the entire crew were all robots, or hypnotized, cheerfully preparing to engage in slaughter for a rotten cause. They had the power, and the terms were rigged in their favor. Freedom, Democracy, Communism, Slavery, Pacification. Anyone in my situation who would argue against the war was obviously just chicken shit. And there was no way out. The system had me, right on the dotted line.

The Executive Officer, the ship's second in command, was a tall Lieutenant Commander with close cropped steel gray hair.

"Why were you absent without leave, sailor?"

The standard answer to that question goes something like this: "Well, Sir, I got drunk, see, and then I was in a motel with this whore, Sir, and the bitch stole my car and..."

What I said was "Well, Sir, I just can't do this any more. I don't want to be a part of..."

"Stand at attention!" the XO said. I did. "Act like a man, not a snot nosed baby. What's the matter with you, don't you have any guts? I'm referring you to Captain's Mast."

The Friday before, I had left the ship with the intention of not returning. I boarded a Greyhound bus for Long Beach and began to contemplate life as a deserter, an underground man. Being a fugitive would be a challenge. I was almost looking forward to it. It never occurred to me, however, to seek out a group like the Quakers that might help me. I went to my brother's house. I talked for several hours with him and his wife, and then with a friend of his, an ex-naval officer who gave me several sensible reasons why I should return to my ship. I would not be technically AWOL until Monday morning. There was still plenty of time to go back.

I did not go. I spent most of Monday walking familiar territory, around downtown Long Beach, and over on the West Side, where I had grown up and where my parents still lived. They didn't even know I was in town. In future, I could only see them furtively, if at all. Nor could I return to Northern California, to my friends, to Mary or Miranda, and to the scenery that I had grown to love. I didn't know where I would go. I assumed that eventually someone would be after me.

On Tuesday afternoon, I put my hated uniform back on. The black shoes, the pants with the silly button flap in front. Thirteen buttons, one for each of the original thirteen states. The jersey with its large, white-bordered collar, the silk tie which I, as a left hander, still couldn't tie properly, and the demeaning little hat. I took the bus to San Diego, and went back to my ship. I had only made it for four days in Montreal, remember? My past, my identity, as confused as it was, was too much to give up. I should have known it all along.

The evening I returned, I was down in my office smoking cigarettes and writing letters. Mr. Hooper came in. To my surprise, he was human and sympathetic, and revealed his own ambivalence about the situation he was in. It was the first crack in the gung-ho shipboard façade that I had seen.

The next day, after I had gone before the XO, Hooper gave me permission to visit the psychiatrist on the base. First, though, I had a session with the Deck Officer, Ensign Maloney. One of his collateral duties was Legal Officer. He was a cheerful, stocky type who had played a little football at Notre Dame. I knew he was trying hard for a transfer to a swift boat, so he could speed around the Mekong Delta with a .45 strapped to his waist and board junks. My case was open and shut. I had been AWOL. No apparent extenuating circumstances. I probably shouldn't try to make a big thing out of it.

The psychiatrist was routine, abrupt. We talked about depression. I thought I was losing control. I explained how life aboard ship seemed unreal, like watching a movie, with me as audience rather than actor.

"Ah!" he said. "But you know it's not a movie, don't you?"

"Yes, but..."

"Then it's nothing serious, okay? You're fit for duty. I'll give you this prescription. Take it back to your ship's corpsman and he'll fill it for you."

He handed me my medical folder, and I left. On the way back to the ship, I read his diagnosis – Adult Situational Reaction. Imagine. The Navy is totally insane, my country is perpetrating a murderous, unjust war, and I, a twenty-two year old kid, can't react to the situation like an adult and just accept it.

I got my pills from the corpsman, little yellow ones, some sort of tranquilizer. The next morning I went to Captain's Mast, held outdoors on a deck near his stateroom. As I stood there with the other offenders, I could look around and see dozens of ships. And the base went on, pier after pier, building after building, as far as the eye could see. Across the harbor, on Coronado Island, Navy jets were taking off and landing almost every minute. Sondberg, the yeoman third class who worked in the ship's office, was standing next to the Captain, taking notes on the proceedings, his glasses sliding down his nose.

When my turn came, and I stood in front of the Captain and saluted him, my knees could not help but shake. Here, with stern gray eyes set in a craggy face, was the fleshly embodiment of all that metallic, immense authority. He looked down at the charge sheet Sondberg set before him on the lectern. After a moment, he looked up.

"AWOL two days, sailor? What happened?"

"It was a mistake, Sir. It won't happen again."

His eyes flashed slightly. He looked over at the Executive Officer, then back at me. "You see that it doesn't, sailor. I'm giving you thirty days hard labor. Dismissed."

21

Thirty days hard labor didn't turn out quite as onerous as it sounded. During the day, I performed my regular office tasks, then after supper had to report to the duty master-at-arms. He had a list of projects and would assign me one. It was the kind of work no one else wanted to do, often in cramped and dirty spaces. I cleaned and painted bilges, scraped and painted musty gear lockers, and wiped accumulated grease off some of the most hard to reach corners of the engine rooms. The physical work was good for me. I slept well. I couldn't go ashore to drink. After a week or so, I stopped taking the little yellow pills.

The last two weeks of my sentence, I worked entirely for the sonar gang, scraping and repainting the inside of a hydraulic chute leading from a depth charge magazine to the firing mechanism on deck. The depth charges, for some reason, were called hedgehogs. The chute had been discovered to be inoperable during the December sea trials. The ASW officer had been reprimanded, the hydraulic mechanism fixed, and new paint ordered.

It was a hell of a job. The chute was hardly big enough for a ladder, a droplight, and me. There was no ventilation. I could imagine the hoist somehow starting up and crushing me to death. There were several coats of paint to be removed. Some layers came off in a fine dust that filled my eyes and nose; other layers were as hard as a rock. I could only work ten or fifteen minutes at a stretch, and then would have to take a break. I couldn't smoke in the magazine, because of the hedgehogs, so I would go down the passageway to the sonar shack. There were usually several people in there, tinkering with the electronic gear, or playing cards. I was supposed to work four hours a night. I fell into a routine of working for about two hours and then playing hearts for an hour or so and knocking off. I finished the work on the chute just as my thirty days were up.

I liked the sonar crew better than the gunner's mates. They were smarter, funnier, less crude. They had fewer tattoos. They were part of Fox Division, along with the fire control technicians. I asked the Weapons Officer if I could switch divisions, and permission was granted shortly before the beginning of March, when the boilers were finally fixed and we left for WESTPAC.

Being AWOL, receiving military justice, doing hard labor, all had a subtle effect. On the one hand, I was adjusting, finding companions, coping with my depression. On the other hand, I had given up something. I had to let go of my righteous indignation, my innocence. I had to accept that I was part of this gigantic murdering machine. The system had beaten me, and made of me what it wanted, and I gave it my obedience, and would have to live with that fact for the rest of my life.

Three

As we left San Diego, I was at my lookout post on the flying bridge and could see everything. We went north up the harbor, leaving pier after pier of naval ships behind. Coronado was to the left, the San Diego skyline to the right. We steered west and then south between North Island Air Station and Point Loma. When we cleared the point, the swells were heavy. We increased speed and the bow spray reached as high as where I was standing. The sea was dark and sparkling, and the sky a brilliant cloudless blue. It was beautiful. I hoped I wouldn't become seasick.

It was a futile hope. For a day and a half, I could leave my bunk only to puke, but I was fine later that week when we reached Pearl Harbor. I looked forward to going ashore. It was the first time I had worn my tropical whites, which consisted of cotton pants and a short-sleeved dress shirt. As the enlisted men went ashore, the officer at the gangplank, Ensign Brock, looked us over carefully. He wouldn't let me off the ship because my belt buckle was, as he put it, "ratty." Here we were, on our way to a watery grave, and me with a ratty belt buckle. Brock was the Radio Officer. I knew he was having some kind of feud with the Weapons Officer, and I figured I was just a pawn. I borrowed a shiny buckle from Josephs and made it off the ship.

We were to be in Honolulu for only one night. I had arranged to visit a good friend from childhood. Irene and her husband Barry worked for an airline, and were hoping to emigrate to Australia. Barry loaned me some clothes. He was four or five inches shorter than I, so the pant legs were at flood level, but it was better than wearing a uniform. They drove me around town, then up to the Pali and out to the Blow Hole.

We drank gin and ate Chinese food. They took me, almost as a joke, to see a happy hula song and dance act in a night club where the stage looked like a grass shack and the drinks looked like tropical lagoons.

The next morning Irene was up at five o'clock to drive me out to Pearl Harbor. She didn't approve of the war any more than I did, but there was still a stereotypical seeing the boys off to the front aspect to our parting. She kissed me, and told me to be brave and be careful, then got back into her yellow Mustang, waved a tanned arm at me, and drove away.

I should describe a few more of these boys I was off to the front with. I worked most closely with Mr. Skelton, the Weapons Officer. Not much older than I, he was an up-and-comer, a hot shot. Though only a Lieutenant Junior Grade, he was filling the billet of a full Lieutenant. He was short, wiry, intense. Raised in Mobile, he had gone to college in Chapel Hill. I saw his wife once, a perfectly coiffed and made up little piece of porcelain with the jitters. Skelton played handball with the Captain from time to time, and once told me that whether he made a career of the Navy depended on what moves Red China made. He knew, however, that his chances for getting to the top were marred because he hadn't gone to Annapolis.

LTJG Hooper, the Gunnery Officer, was a different story. Chubby and easygoing, he was from Cleveland and had gone to Ohio State. He was looking forward to leaving the Navy so he could enter law school. We were about as friendly as officer and enlisted man could be under the circumstances. We joked sometimes in the privacy of the weapons office and could be honest about our feelings toward what went on around us.

As for the crew, some had brains and some didn't. Many were overweight. Some were devout Christians; some were profane whoremongers. Some were both. All were cogs in a great imperial adventure. Some knew it; some didn't. Some were short timers, and some were lifers.

I know it is unfair, but when I think of lifers, I always think of Burford, a pot-bellied second class gunner's mate, and of the morning in Hong Kong when he came in to complain to the Weapons Officer about all the useless armor piercing shells we had taken aboard in Japan, which would be no good at all for shooting gooks out of trees. He wound up showing Mr. Skelton some snapshots of his kids, and that night on the shuttle launch back to the ship I heard him drunkenly brag that he had just had a blow job from a ten-year-old girl on the rooftops of Wanchai.

Then there were the odd ones, the losers. There was one deck hand with an unpronounceable German name that sounded a little like honeybucket, so everyone called him Honeybucket. He was a pale myopic slug from the Oregon coast. He had enlisted because the recruiter told him he could probably play his cello in the Navy's symphony orchestra. The Navy had no symphony orchestra. Honeybucket had one of those crew cuts that went every which way, and his glasses were always covered with greasy fingerprints. He tended to drool, and almost never bathed. From time to time the other deck apes would throw him in the shower and work him over with a scrub brush. He was the best chess player on board ship.

His counterpart down in the boiler room was a fireman named Young. His hair also never stayed combed, his glasses were always smeared, and he seemed allergic to soap. He didn't drool, but he did stutter, and became thereby the butt of many jokes. He wasn't much good at anything.

The enlisted men I worked most closely with were the other yeomen. The Engineering Yeoman had a little office right across from mine. He was a complainer. A reservist like I was, he had a year of college and was classified as a journalist. He had a standard, almost daily litany of how his talents were being wasted, and how he should be working in Public Information on a carrier or in Honolulu. He was always writing letters requesting a transfer. He also complained about the food, the crew, the officers, his hard bunk, and the often faulty air conditioning.

The ship's main office was headed by a chief personnelman who drank too much when ashore and spent most of the time in his bunk when he was aboard. There were two yeoman strikers, seamen. Matowski was a street kid from Milwaukee. Jefferson, who aside from one of the cooks was the only African-American on the ship not assigned to the engine or boiler rooms, was from Denver. He was the other flying bridge lookout on my sea and anchor detail, and we wound up spending a lot of time together.

And then there was Lars Sondberg, a third class yeoman. The night after leaving Honolulu, he stopped by me as I was sitting on a winch on the fantail, smoking and being mesmerized by the ship's wake. He apologized for not having been very friendly before. He had grown up in San Diego, and when there lived at home with his mother and brother, and had as little as possible to do with the Navy. He thought, though, that we might have a lot in common. And he was right. Tall, lanky, and unkempt, he was cynical, funny, well read, had seen even more foreign films than I had, and loved to discuss them. Both his parents had been raised in a failed utopia in the mountains east of San Diego and, though "uneducated," had provided him with a stimulating home life. One of his aunts had a Ph.D. from Benares, and owned an esoteric bookstore in Santa Monica. His father, a printer, had died when Lars was a college freshman, leaving him financially and emotionally adrift. He had joined the Navy for four years, and regretted it, though he had spent two years ashore in Honolulu. He had one more year to serve.

We were to spend most of our leisure hours together, many of them down in my office. Together, we smoked a million cigarettes, drank ten thousand cups of lousy coffee, and watched, with jaded eye, the deadly progress of an auxiliary war effort.

We docked in Yokosuka, Japan, and spent two days bringing aboard supplies and ammunition. Boxes and metal shell containers were stacked on pallets on the pier, and we carried them aboard like a string of coolies. After the first morning, Honeybucket was not allowed to carry ammunition. Twice he let a heavy shell slip from his grasp and bounce on the deck, scaring the bejeezus out of everyone around him.

Then it was Sunday, and liberty began at ten a.m. I took the train over to Kamakura to see the great Buddha. I vaguely recall that you could walk up inside him, but I mostly remember sitting on a bench in the garden, looking up at the statue. The garden was crowded, but compared to my ship seemed serene and spacious. I was the only sailor and only Caucasian there.

From Kamakura, I took a rickety local to the island of Eno Shima, and had some good views of Fuji on the way. The carriage had what I would call a sour scotch smell, and reminded me of the way my first love's mouth would sometimes taste in the morning when we woke up.

I had been drinking in some of the bars around Yokosuka the two previous evenings, and had seen my first Asian bar girls. Some of them were very attractive. One I talked to, who was with one of the sonar gang, even claimed to be studying English literature in college. But they were all still prostitutes. I had had your standard puritanical upbringing, full of cautionary tales of bodies rotting away with venereal disease. A residue of that puritanism remained, but was layered with other considerations. These women were exploited, economically and sexually, and my conscience could not ignore that. I had a certain sense of feminist issues, about as much as an immature American male could have had in 1966. That first love affair had been helped to its demise by my adolescent preoccupation with the rites of frequent sex. I had been blind to other important things, but sadly learned a sort of lesson. A bit later, I had read Doris Lessing's *Golden Notebook*, another taste of the impending gender sea changes.

Above all, I didn't want to be like the rest of the sailors: randy, willing to screw anything that walked, sickeningly racist. Slants, crosscunts, were all whores. You could do things to them you wouldn't dare to do to a broad back home.

28

There can be sex without war, but apparently no war without sex. The stories I heard, though, didn't make it sound like very good sex. One young gunner talked of being fucked, drunk, standing up against an alley wall in Yokosuka, having to take the old whore's word for it that he had come, and they were finished. Maybe there *were* a million sailors out there, who kept their mouths shut, who didn't think too much and were having a great, satisfying time. But I doubted that it would work for me. What I wanted to happen, of course, was to be with Miranda, a Miranda who returned my affection, or her Asian equivalent, a woman of beauty and charm, someone I could talk to. Then, whatever happened would flow from attraction and love of life, not from a drunken cash transaction.

What did happen was that I walked around Eno Shima, a beautiful traffic-free island marred only by too many souvenir shops, and drank beer in a little café with a juke box, and played the Beatles over and over again, much to the delight of a group of teenagers who danced and danced and thanked me every time I put more coins in. I asked one of them to write the word "Beatles" for me in Japanese. I was fond of that little slip of paper and kept it in my wallet until I eventually lost it.

In Hong Kong, in a restaurant on Victoria Island, I met an Australian. He was thin, dignified, well dressed, with white hair. About fifty, I would say. He asked to join me at my table, and in his nasal accent put friendly, innocent questions to me about my ship, what my various insignia meant, my duties, where we were going, etc. Exactly the kind of information we had been warned not to discuss. I felt silly evading his questions, but did so anyway. When I was finished with my meal he bought me a beer, and for reasons I still don't understand, told me what follows.

"I was an upright man," he said, "and proud of myself. I worked for a well-known publisher, as a text book salesman. I had a house in the Sydney suburbs, a car, a wife, two nearly grown children. I felt I was doing my duty in the world.

"I won't bore you with the details, but one day two years ago I had a revelation, like Saul on the road to Damascus. I saw that I had wasted my life. And do you know why? Altruism! It's a form of hypocrisy, you know. I had lived for the good of others, and was an empty hollow shell.

"I threw it all over, and moved here to Hong Kong. I deal high risk stocks and bonds. I'm a good salesman, if I do say so myself, and make a great deal of money. I have a penthouse apartment and a young Chinese mistress. The only thing worth living for, my friend, is pure selfishness. Otherwise, you just rot away inside."

He wished me good luck and left. I ran into him on the street in Kowloon a few nights later, after I had my civilian clothes. He was with a Caucasian woman about his own age. "Ah," he said, "your suit looks quite nice. When you told me about it, I was afraid they might have sold you something outlandishly garish." I don't know how he could tell, as we were standing in a circle of yellow light cast by a large neon sign above us. He passed a few more pleasantries, and then he and the woman continued on their way. Maybe he was a spy. Maybe he was the Devil. Maybe he was just a middle aged Australian.

We were lucky. We were to be in Hong Kong three weeks, as a sort of radio central for all the U.S. warships in the Far East. Liberty usually began at noon. The first day, when you stepped from the shuttle onto the pier, several smiling men approached you with business cards for local tailors. I visited one, who served free beer while I was being fitted. Enlisted men were not allowed to wear civilian clothes in WESTPAC. I no longer cared. My suit would be ready in three days.

The cheapest place to drink was at the British Armed Forces Club. You talked to some interesting types there and had a raffish pukka sahib last days of the empire sort of time. The British tars were jolly and jealous; we were on our way to a bit of the real thing while they polished bloody brass. I spent most of my time in that club until my suit was ready.

I kept the suit in a locker at the Kowloon YMCA, along with the shirt, tie, belt, and shoes I had bought to go with it. Suitably dressed, I would walk over to the lounge of the vice-regal, posh Peninsula Hotel to drink tea and read the newspaper. I felt Victorian, civilized, and enjoyed the cricket match articles filled with Chinese names. I liked to drink next door to the Peninsula, in the penthouse bar of the President Hotel. I would sit near a window writing long letters and watching the lights twinkle in the harbor. Then I would wander out and eat like a lonely king, for even the fancy restaurants were inexpensive, and I developed a taste for shark fin soup. I had supper with Sondberg once, but he spent most of his time with a certain young lady in a bar in Wanchai.

My evenings all ended the same way. A drink or two, then back to the YMCA to don my uniform and my misgivings, then the Star Ferry across to Victoria to wait at the liberty boat dock with other drunken sailors, listen to their swagger and pugnaciousness, then chug chug back to the ship, take one last look at the marvelous twinkling lights of the colony, and so to a dark sleep.

After Hong Kong, we stopped for a few days at Subic Bay in the Philippines. We off-loaded most of the armor piercing shells we had picked up in Japan, trading them for fragmentation rounds. I did not visit the nearby town of Olongapo, having been told nothing was there but a dusty, bar lined street. I drank San Miguel beer at the Enlisted Men's Club on the base, and listened to an awful rock band. The beer had a bitter taste. I was told that because of the climate and polluted water supply, the brewers always put a little formaldehyde in it.

When we left Subic, we had a day of target practice, shooting at a small, uninhabited island. It was a restricted area, and off limits to the Filipinos, but as we were firing, someone noticed a man close to shore in a small canoe, paddling like mad. We ceased firing until he was away from the range. A lot of people thought he looked quite funny, paddling like that, so scared and all.

31

Four

We arrived off the coast of South Vietnam about nine in the morning, and two thousand yards offshore we went to general quarters. All hands manned their battle stations. The guns were ready for loading. The watertight hatches were secured to contain any flooding if we sustained a hit. The torpedoes, depth charges, and hedgehogs were operational. The fire hoses were unrolled. An officer was positioned in front of the ship's safe with a loaded .45, and the corpsman sat in the sick bay ready to receive the wounded.

All personnel with topside battle stations were wearing helmets and flak jackets. They were heavy and made you sweat. Clyde, a Georgia farm boy on my gun crew, had a helmet that kept slipping down over his eyes, and he kept pushing it back up. We could see a small fishing village on the beach. "Is them Communist houses?" he asked, and I tried to set him straight.

And then we waited; waited for orders from forward spotters ashore, who crouched in trees looking through binoculars, or circled above the action in helicopters or small planes. What we were, after all, was a floating gun platform. NGFS, they called it, Naval Gun Fire Support. The Buckett had three five-inch mounts, one forward and two aft. They vaguely resembled the head of an elephant with an erected trunk. The barrel was over twenty feet in length, the shells were five inches in diameter, about three feet long, and weighed seventy pounds. These guns could fire twenty rounds a minute and had a range of about five miles.

My gun was one of the smaller ones, three inchers, one forward and one aft. They each had two barrels and could fire fifty rounds a minute. The shells weighed only seven pounds and were loaded into the gun by hand, whereas the five-inch guns were loaded by a mechanism that frequently broke down. The five-inch guns, from forward to aft, were designated mounts 51, 52, and 53. The three-inch guns were likewise 31 and 32. My gun, 32, was up on the 02 deck, crammed between Mount 52 and an ammunition magazine.

We waited some more. It was hot. There was no wind. The helmets and flak jackets grew ever more uncomfortable. They seemed unnecessary. Who was going to shoot at us, the Viet Cong Navy? The officers on the bridge may have known what was going on, but nobody told us. Clyde needed to pee. Josephs called up to the bridge for permission for him to do so. It was granted. Later, I was sent down to the Weapons Office, unscrewing a watertight hatch to do so, in order to take a certain manual up to the bridge. By now, we had the flak jackets unzipped and the helmets in our laps and were sitting around wherever there was shade.

It was past noon, and the crew was hungry. We secured from general quarters for lunch. The spotter said it was okay. Fifteen minutes later, while most of us were still waiting in the mess line, general quarters sounded again. Four rounds were fired off into the jungle, and then we waited another hour before we finally had our lunch.

That evening, after supper, we went to general quarters again. It had been a beautiful sunset. I was used to being on land and watching the sun set into the sea. It was very different to be on the ocean and see the glow fade behind the low hills.

"This is the Captain speaking," the loudspeaker blared. Maybe he would let us know what was going on. "Forward Air Spotter has a communist supply caravan, about a hundred VC and several elephants. We're preparing to fire at this time." Two of the five-inch guns opened up, and about sixty rounds were fired.

"This is the Captain speaking," we heard again. "The spotter reports several direct hits. Good job, well done."

Clyde was pensive, leaning back against the bulkhead of the magazine. I thought he had some tears in his eyes.

"Poor ol' elephants," he said.

You tell me. I had never heard of the NLF using elephants. Was it true, or was some spotter drunk, out there, sitting in his tree? Did he like pulling jokes on the Navy? Or maybe it was the Captain, trying to liven things up for us. In any case, elephants or no, there were still those hundred or so VC and those several direct hits. I didn't want to think about it.

Because of their longer range, most of the firing was done by the five-inch guns. We were on line three days before Mount 32 saw any action. We had been at GQ most of a muggy afternoon. I was reading; Clyde was asleep. The others were smoking and telling lies. By now, general quarters had become a fairly sloppy affair. It didn't make much sense to worry about watertight hatches, torpedoes, hoses, or preparing to care for the wounded. Orders to fire were passed down, and we had to hustle to load the barrels. Clyde was little help. He seemed still half-asleep, as if he wasn't sure where he was.

We fired about forty rounds, and then we ceased firing, and I sat in some shade looking at the coastline and thinking how tired I was. I looked at my hands. There was a long scratch on one of my thumbs, but it wasn't bleeding. Clyde closed his eyes and headed back into dreamland. The others picked up their conversation where it had been interrupted.

"This is the Captain speaking," came that voice again. "Good job, Mount 32. The spotter reports several enemy KIA. Well done."

"Hey, fuckin' all right," said Josephs, and most of the others chimed in.

So there it was. I had put shells in a big gun, and the shells had killed people. Good job, well done. A year earlier I would have thought it impossible, but the way had been comprised of so many small steps that when it finally came, it hardly seemed like a line had been crossed at all.

34

Mount 53 wasn't very reliable, and seemed to be down more than its share of the time. The mechanisms of these miracles of technology were extremely complex. A little switch or fuse or spring would go bad and the gun would simply be unable to fire. Once we didn't even have the necessary repair part on board ship, and a helicopter had to fly out from somewhere and drop a tiny box on the fantail. That was the kind of thing that made a ship and its crew look sloppy.

Murchison was in charge of Mount 53. He spent long hours trying to keep the gun on line; lack of sleep made the little craters in his face blotchy. His gloom cloud grew larger and darker, and he developed some sort of tic in his right eye. When the gun was down, the Captain would express his displeasure, and the XO would pass it on to the Weapons Officer, and Skelton would pass it on to the Gunnery Officer, and Hooper would have to go look over Murchison's shoulder, and Murchison would be crouched down somewhere trying to fix a fuse and his fingers would start to fumble even more and he'd wonder once again why nothing ever seemed to go right in his life. Finally, Mr. Skelton switched him up to Mount 52, which had the best record for reliability. Burford moved back from 52 to 53, and the gun worked pretty well after that.

Our war was erratic, boring, exhausting. After a week of general quarters, a schedule had been devised which kept one five-inch mount always manned, but freed most of the crew for their normal duties. One third of us were on watch at any one time. You stood four hours on, eight hours off, unless you had the dog watch from six to eight p.m., a device which allowed the sections to rotate so a person wasn't always stuck, say, on the midnight to four a.m. watch. The ship's bells were inexorable. If you were unlucky, you might work all day, be at GQ all evening, stand a midnight to four a.m. watch, grab two hours of sleep, and be on duty all next day. Everyone was tired, many were irritable, and there was no end of griping.

My watch was the same as on the sea and anchor detail: port lookout on the flying bridge. I loved it, being up there in the air and sun or stars, smoking and watching the sea. My starboard companion was a short, simian deck ape named Pedrelli. He almost never spoke, which suited me just fine. Jefferson, for instance, would have talked my ear off and bored me silly.

I was a good lookout, and usually spotted planes or small boats or objects in the water before the officers on the bridge did. I was an accurate judge of distance also, and often placed a small boat within one or two hundred yards of what the radar calculated. Unfortunately, the junior officer on the bridge during my watch was Ensign Brock. He liked to be tricky, especially at night. I would be standing there, musing, and suddenly his voice would blast over my headphones. "Bridge to port lookout. What's that light in the sky at 240 degrees? Why didn't you report it?"

"I'd say it's a star, Sir."

"Just keeping you on your toes, Feldkirchen."

Once we had a day off. A beat up old landing craft appeared from God knows where, filled with dozens of cases of warm beer. We went over the side in shifts, standing unsteadily on the deck of the landing craft, guzzling as fast as we could until the next shift replaced us. When the party was over and we steamed slowly away, hundreds of beer cans floated, like a toy armada, on the untroubled surface of the sea.

After thirty days on line we returned to Subic Bay for two weeks of maintenance and fun. The Enlisted Men's Club had the same bitter San Miguel beer and the same lousy rock band. One night when Sondberg had the duty, I went with Matowski, the yeoman striker from Milwaukee, to a special recreation spot on an island somewhere. I think it was still part of the American base; a landing craft made a regular run there. It was a pleasant little island, with sandy beaches and palm trees and hamburgers and cheap drinks. Matowski and I drank gin.

There were some girls there from a school run by the Methodists. They sat demurely in chairs along the wall, waiting patiently never to be asked to dance.

The Buckett's Executive Officer came in, accompanied by the Supply Officer. They nodded to us and sat at a table across the room. After a while Matowski said, "Let's buy them a drink."

"All right," I said.

Later, they returned the favor, and Matowski waved thanks to them. Then he went off to the bathroom somewhere. He came back with a copy of *Newsweek*. On the cover was a clean-cut kid on a motorcycle, a little Honda or something, and sitting behind him was a sweet young thing with long blonde hair.

"Look at that," he said, pointing a weaving finger at the cover. "Look at that. That's all a person needs in life. That's all I want, anyway. Just a bike and a chick. A bike and a chick, and a good job somewhere. That's freedom, brother." He was almost in tears. "All my life, that's all I wanted, just a bike and a chick. No old man beating the shit out of you, no fucking filthy sidewalks, just a bike and a chick and away you go."

"How old are you?" I asked.

"Nineteen," he said, and I tried, tipsily, to tell him what it had been like back when I was nineteen. Later, I went to the bathroom, and after I came back the waitress arrived and said the gentlemen were sorry, but they couldn't accept the drinks, as they were leaving. I looked over and the XO was gone.

"Did you buy them another drink?" I asked.

"Yeah."

"Shit," I said, "they didn't even deserve the first one."

So there we were. We each had a gin, and also now had a scotch and something elegant with a cherry in it. I drank the gins and Matowski finished the other two. I leafed through the *Newsweek* and came across a picture of an ignited Vietnamese monk, but decided not to show it to Matowski. We left, and stood on the pier waiting for the landing craft to shuttle us home. We looked at the stars. As we chugged across the channel, Matowski was sick. He tried to stand on the seat and puke over the side, but the bulkhead was too high and the puke ran down the inside and collected in a puddle on the bench. I had to carry him onto the ship. The next morning the XO ordered Mr. Skelton to give me a little talk on setting a good moral example. Skelton had Hooper do it.

Olongapo looked pretty much as it had been described: a long dirt road lined with bars, wooden sidewalks, and buildings all up on posts. I went over there with Sondberg and a couple of others. We found a fairly good restaurant and ate fish and got drunk on white wine. Then we rode in a jitney somewhere where the roads were paved and there was a large dance hall all lit in a soft eerie blue and the bar girls fluttered around trying to join us, but we didn't have enough money left and shooed them away. Maybe it was all a dream.

I went back to the restaurant a few days later, alone, for the white wine and shark fin soup. Afterwards, I walked along the wooden sidewalk, wanting more to drink. There was a place called the Frisco Bay. I was navigating through the crowded tables toward a barstool when a woman sitting at one of the tables grabbed my arm. She was very pretty. "Hey Joe," she said, "I love you, no shit. Buy me drink." It was the standard line. I sat down and we drank and talked. I must have bought us each about six drinks, and spent over twenty dollars. She drank little shot glasses of something; I thought it might be tea and made her give me a taste. It was brandy. I couldn't figure out how old she was, and she wouldn't tell me. She did tell me about the village where she had been a little girl, and we talked about rain, and mud, and pigs and heat and palm trees and beautiful sunsets. I told her why there was no point in wearing my suit in Olongapo, because of Auden's *Musée des Beaux Arts*. We agreed that we both liked poetry. I told her about how Edward Trelawny put his hand into the fire of Shelley's funeral pyre and plucked out the heart, later giving it to Mary Shelley, who dried it and kept it flattened in a copy of *Adonais,* where it remained until it was buried with her in Bournemouth.

Now there were different colored lights, and people dancing, and loud country and western music. My friend was not only pretty and poetic but also mysterious and alluring. It was still early, and I didn't have to be back to the ship until midnight. A little voice inside my head made it across the buzz and I heard it say "All is Possible." I asked the woman to dance.

She couldn't have been more than four-foot-six. She came up to just below my solar plexus. I looked down and there, in the distance, was the top of her head, her dark hair parted neatly in the middle.

"Actually," I said, "I don't feel very much like dancing." We sat back down and had one more quiet drink, and then I excused myself and took a jitney back to the base.

We returned to Vietnam, and they kept us busy. Now it was Mount 52 that most often developed problems. Murchison spent all of his time trying to keep it working, and retreated further and further into himself. He would hardly talk to anyone, and when he did he usually confined himself to strange sayings or bitter complaints. One night he came down to the Weapons Office to look at a reference manual and found me sitting there, my feet up on my desk, reading, smoking, and drinking coffee. "Get off your ass and get busy," he told me, the tic in his eye working overtime.

"Murchison," I said, "It's eleven o'clock at night!"

"You punks get away with everything," he said.

Whenever a gun was inoperable, you had to send a status report to the flotilla commander letting him know its condition and how long it would take to fix. It embarrasses the Captain and others to have to keep sending these things in, especially if the repair time is longer than the original estimate, and they have to go back and revise it. The reports are important, though, as they help the powers-that-be decide what ship to send where.

39

One day, with all the guns on line, we were ordered to a spot that needed as many rounds as we could give, as fast as we could give them. All five guns were firing, and then Mount 52 went down. Hooper came back for a hurried conference with Murchison, then went up to report to the bridge. I didn't see it, but I heard that the Captain just blew up. "That Murchison is making me the fool of the fleet," he supposedly said. "You tell him he's got six hours to get that mount fixed or he's off the guns for good! Send Burford in to help him."

We soon broke from GQ, and things were fairly quiet except for the comings and goings around Mount 52. A few hours later, the gun was still down, but Murchison and Burford broke for evening chow. They sat there at a table in the middle of the mess deck, Murchison completely enveloped in his dark cumulus, shoving food in with his right hand while his left, white-knuckled, clutched the table. Honeybucket came along and set his tray down opposite him. He didn't seem to notice Murchison's mood; maybe his glasses were too smeared to tell. He wiped off some drool with his sleeve, and shoveled in half a biscuit. Chewing with his mouth open, he looked up at Murchison.

"Got'cher gun workin'?" he asked.

In about two seconds Murchison had Honeybucket on the deck, and Burford and two others were pulling him off by the arms and neck and trying to hold him down. Then he just collapsed and started to sob and make little blubbering sounds. Honeybucket scooted backwards until he collided with a bulkhead. "What did I do?" he asked, looking around for his glasses, and somebody got him the hell out, fast. Then the XO was there, in stockinged feet and undershirt, holding his khaki shirt in one hand. Murchison was curled up on the floor, still sobbing. The XO put on his shirt and buttoned it, and tucked it into his pants.

"Have the corpsman report to the mess deck," he ordered.

Murchison spent the next few days in sick bay, under heavy sedation. Then they tapered off the dose so he could walk, and soon a helicopter arrived from somewhere and lowered a new man onto the deck. He was a second class gunner's mate; Burford had known him well on a previous ship. Murchison was brought out to the fantail and put in the little saddle. The helicopter reeled him up and whooshed away. He was in the hospital in Subic for a while and then was flown back to the states. No one heard what became of him after that.

One afternoon, during a slow GQ, I was sitting in the gunner's seat, reading *Alice in Wonderland*. It was a fine day, almost cool. I heard a whirring sound and looked up to see Mr. Hooper shooting at me with a super 8 camera he had bought in Hong Kong. "Hey," I shouted, jumping down behind the mount. He stopped filming and I stood up. "What if they have a war crimes trial when this is all over? That could be used in evidence against me!" He laughed, and had me film him in front of the gun.

A short while later the three-inchers were ordered to fire. Clyde was busily filling my hopper, and I was stuffing round after round into the chamber, but out of the corner of my eye I could see Hooper whirring away, getting some great action shots. He's probably an overweight, successful attorney these days. Somewhere, in Cleveland or wherever he lives, there may well be some fading rolls of film stuffed away in a drawer, like a guilty conscience, gathering dust.

Sometimes it would be so dark you couldn't see a thing. It was three a.m., and I was on watch, looking into the nothingness. Without notice a round was fired from the forward five-inch gun. The flash, in the same instant that it momentarily blinded me, revealed a bumboat about five yards from the bow. For a confused second I thought it had mined us or something. Crouching, sightless, I called the bridge. "There's a bumboat with two men in it right off the port bow!"

"Which way is it heading?"

"I don't know," I answered, "the flash blinded me. Why didn't you warn us about that round?"

"Sorry about that," Brock said. They turned a spotlight on the area, but the boat was gone. It was probably fishermen, drifting, asleep, and I'm sure when the round went off they were more frightened than I was.

Pedrelli, to starboard, spoke up that night, one of the few times he ever said a thing to me during our months of watching together. "You know," he said, "sometimes being out here makes you feel a little crazy." We never did hear why that round had been fired.

Five

Kaohsiung is a large port city on the southern tip of Taiwan. The harbor entrance was extremely narrow, flanked by ancient battlements. The Buckett seemed barely able to squeak through. The harbor itself, though, was large enough to moor scores of rusty crumbling freighters, a dozen American destroyers, some small ships of the Generalissimo's Navy, and innumerable bumboats flitting here and there like water spiders, collecting cargo or garbage, offering laundry service or cheap watches to the American crews, or having no apparent purpose at all.

We moored in the middle of the harbor. This was true R&R, a hot and humid sailor's paradise. Liberty began at noon. A shuttle boat took you to a pier where the main street began. After a half mile of drab warehouses, that road in the next mile held probably two hundred bars. They had the same quaint names as the sailor joints all over Asia: The Pussycat, Busy Beaver, Alamo, etc. There was one called the First Bar, which did a flourishing business as thirsty sailors jumped into taxis at the pier and said "Take me to the first bar!" They began to worry when the taxi seemed to be heading past their hearts' desire, but when it arrived and the driver pointed to the neon sign, they thought it was a great joke and went on in.

The traffic was incomprehensible. There were dogs and goats, and people carrying heavy sacks or pushing handcarts. There were rickshaws, motor scooters, taxis, pickups, and heavy trucks. Uniformed soldiers with machine guns stood on every corner, but there were no stoplights and no apparent rules of the road. The taxis cruised at about thirty-five, horns blaring, apparently not equipped with brakes. The hordes in the streets seemed oblivious to them, but at the last second would miraculously part, like the Red Sea, and the taxis would glide through.

I was finally ready for prostitutes, for something, anything besides gray steel. I don't remember how Sondberg and I chose the bar we did. Perhaps we just asked the driver for the prettiest girls, and this bar, the Do Re Mi, happened to be owned by his cousin. It was dark inside, and fairly empty.

My girl was called Suzie. Sondberg's was Lonnie. Suzie was eighteen or nineteen, pretty, quiet, almost demure. Her face had a peasant broadness and openness which I assumed was Taiwanese as opposed to the more delicate mainland features. She had full lips and a beautiful smile. Lonnie was older, brasher, funnier, and more sophisticated. She liked to punch people playfully in the stomach.

Suzie's story, which I pieced together over the next week, was perhaps true. She came from a poor village; her parents were dead. Her uncle hadn't exactly sold her to a slaver, but money had changed hands. The slaver put her in the care of the Do Re Mi's Mamasan, a pleasant overweight woman of about forty. Mamasan taught her the trade, but didn't teach her until later about contraception, and she had a son when she was sixteen. Mamasan paid for things, and supported mother and child until Suzie could return to work, saddled with a large debt which she had to stay at the Do Re Mi to repay.

The drinks were expensive. The girls wondered what kind of cars we owned, and what we did on board ship. We didn't own cars, and wouldn't tell them about our work, accusing them of being spies. It was nice to have someone to touch.

Lars and I wanted a good meal for a change. We asked the girls to take us to a nice restaurant, one preferably out of town, as we also wanted a ride in the country. The girls seemed strangely uneasy about this. They conversed intently in Chinese, consulted Mamasan, and kept stalling us, having us buy more drinks. But the tipsier we became, the more we wanted to go for supper in the country. Finally they agreed, but said we had to talk to Mamasan first. We had to pay seven dollars each to take them out of the bar, to cover profits lost in their absence. No big deal; we were flush with combat pay.

They took us a few miles out of town, to a golf course or something, part of a USO club maybe, where there was an almost empty hot dog parlor.

"But this isn't what we wanted! We wanted good Chinese food!"

"You wanted Chinese food? How we supposed to know?"

They said there was nowhere else to go, so we stayed and ate hot dogs and drank beer and played pinball machines. Suzie was good, and beat us all. Later that week I heard a story from other sailors, how they had taken their girls to the beach and a crowd of Chinese had thrown sand on the girls and spit at them. No wonder Suzie and Lonnie didn't take us somewhere nice.

About nine o'clock we wanted to be somewhere private, like back at their apartment. We had to be aboard ship at midnight. Lonnie called a taxi, but it didn't arrive for almost two hours, during which time Lars and I fretted and had her call again and drank more beer and finally waved farewell to bedded bliss for that night. We had fun, though, kissing and fondling the women on the taxi ride back to town.

"You come tomorrow," Suzie said. "We go see movie. You my nice sailor boy." Back on board ship, Lars and I realized we had spent about half a month's pay.

The next day after lunch, Lars and I went to the Enlisted Men's Club to drink scotch cheaply, then went to a record stall. The Taiwanese pirated albums, and mass produced them in colorful transparent plastic. They sold for fifteen to twenty cents each. I bought all the Beatles, Bob Dylan, and Joan Baez they had, about ten albums. Then we went to the Do Re Mi. Suzie and Lonnie had been waiting hours! We had the few obligatory drinks, paid Mamasan to let the girls out, and took a taxi a few blocks down the road to the theater.

What we saw first was their National Anthem. Rather, we heard the National Anthem and saw Chiang Kai-shek

45

sitting there in full uniform, beaming at us. Then shots of tanks roaring across country, knocking down fences and trees. Then we saw planes flying in close formation, and artillery explosions and The Flag waving proudly in the sky and back to Chiang smiling benevolently from a massive desk that was almost as polished as his bald head. While this went on, the audience stood reverently at attention.

The movie was *My Fair Lady*, with Chinese subtitles. Suzie mouthed the words of every song, and I wondered numbly how many times she had seen the film. Was this, then, her grand fantasy, that some day a sailor would come into the Do Re Mi and take her off to a world of aristocratic sparkle? And did she think that I might be a candidate?

I had to go to the men's room. I went out to the lobby and down a flight of stairs and, as I entered where the urinals were, I was almost knocked over by the smell. It wasn't just piss, or years of piss, or poverty or bad diet. Somehow, I knew, it was the smell of fear, the chemistry of living under the Generalissimo, of seeing a machine gun on every corner, of waiting for the day when eight hundred million Mainland Chinese squash you like a bug.

After the movie we all wanted supper. They took us to a crowded restaurant three doors down from the Do Re Mi. The owner, they said, was a relative of Mamasan. I had been carrying my records around all afternoon, and as we waited for our food, showed them to Suzie. She liked the Beatles, but had never heard of Joan Baez or Dylan. She had a record player back at her apartment, though, and we could listen to them.

"Can we buy some beer somewhere?" Lars asked.

"Sure, back at the Do Re Mi."

We went back there and all had a drink and Mamasan brought us out two six packs. We started to leave, and she said we had to buy the girls out first.

"But we already did that, this afternoon!"

"That was this afternoon. This is tonight." We paid, but with little grace.

Lonnie and Suzie lived in what must have been the real downtown of Kaohsiung. There were large department stores and other buildings four or five stories tall. Their apartment was long and narrow, on the third floor. It had a kitchen with a balcony, a bathroom, and two small bedrooms. The record player was in Suzie's room. It was cheap plastic with orange knobs and a built-in speaker. We drank beer and listened to some of the albums. Suzie and Lonnie chattered and made it hard to hear. Then Lonnie and Lars went into Lonnie's room. I sat on the bed next to Suzie and started kissing her. I pulled her down next to me and we kissed some more and I felt her breasts through her clothes and then started to take her blouse off, but she wouldn't let me.

"I have period," she said. "You know what period is?"

Yes, I said, I knew what period was, and I sat up and opened another beer.

"You very nice boy."

I put on *Rubber Soul*, which was a bright transparent red, playing the side that began with "Drive my Car" and "Norwegian Wood." Suzie listened, and snapped her fingers and smiled at me, and we kissed some more. Later, I went along the hall to the bathroom, and then stood on the kitchen balcony, looking down into the alley below. The hot air smelled like garbage. In the alley, visible in the light from the ground floor windows, was the largest rat I have ever seen. It looked as big as a cocker spaniel. It was just sitting there, on its haunches. I finished my beer, and threw the empty can down at the rat. I missed by about eight inches. The rat didn't move a muscle, but slowly turned its head and glared up at me. I was damned glad I wasn't down in that alley.

It was about time to leave. Lars came out of Lonnie's room, looking disheveled. We finished the last beers and kissed the girls good-bye and went down to find a taxi. Riding back to the pier, Lars looked over at me and asked "So?"

"Nothing happened," I said.

"Me neither."

47

The next day I was duty yeoman and had to stay aboard ship. The day after that, Lars had the duty and I went alone to the Do Re Mi. Some of the girls were sitting at a table on the sidewalk, playing a game with little wooden cards. Suzie wasn't there.

"Her baby sick, bad sick. She be here tonight, maybe."

Yeah, I thought, I bet her baby is sick. I hadn't seen any signs of a baby at her apartment. Suzie probably got bought last night by some paunchy tattooed sailor, one not about to take no crap about no period. I walked aimlessly along the crowded sidewalk, past the tons of junk displayed for sale there: cowboy hats and shirts, transistor radios, cameras, watches, dragon jackets, kimonos, pornographic books. Some of the bars had a man on the street who took your elbow and began to describe the pleasures to be found inside. At others, the whores themselves sat listlessly at little tables outside or slumped against the sweating walls and called out to you.

"Hey sailor, you want good time? You buy me drink, maybe I give you blow job! You like pussy? Hey sailor, where you go? Come back! You want fuck little boy in asshole?" Then three or four of them would cut loose with a high pitched, mocking cackle.

I went into the Enlisted Men's Club and sat alone and drank several scotches, then went out on the street again. I ran into Mr. Hooper, who had MP duty. His little red arm band kept falling off, because he couldn't bend his arm up enough to tie it with both hands, so I tied it for him and continued along the street. I arrived at what seemed a main crossroad, and walked down half a block or so. It seemed less garish here, quieter. A sign said "Hotel, Restaurant, Bar." I was hungry and went inside. I drank scotch and ate Chop Suey, and shortly a woman joined me. She was slim and fine boned, with a pretty but wasted face. She looked about thirty-five. We drank more scotch, and it seemed to me we were talking high philosophical stuff like the meaning of life and the need for beauty, and that she was keeping up her end of the

48

conversation fairly well. I kept seeing couples go up the stairs. "There's a hotel up there, right?"

"Right," she answered.

"Do any of the rooms have bathtubs? I haven't seen a bathtub in three months."

"You want take bath?"

"Yes, I want a hot, hot bath, and I want you to give me a back rub."

"That all you want?"

"Yes, that's all I want."

So she took a room for us, half price, and we went upstairs and I had a hot, hot bath and tried to soak away the gray steel, while she sat on the bed and looked at a glossy Chinese magazine. This was almost like the real world, and I decided that of course I wanted to sleep with her; she was a nice woman, she knew all about the meaning of life and beauty, and here we were in a cozy room and I didn't have a rubber, couldn't stand the things and so what if I caught VD, that was tomorrow. Now I just wanted to screw, and screw, and screw, and lose myself completely.

I surfaced from the bath and dried off and lay on the bed, where she gave me a back rub. Then I pulled her down beside me and began to kiss her and take off her clothes. She had a lovely body. It looked ten years younger than her face. I snuggled next to her and began to kiss her breasts. She wrapped her fingers lightly around my penis. After a few seconds, I started to come.

"Hey," she said angrily, even before the first waves had subsided, "what you do that for?"

"Well..." I said.

"Why you mess bed all up? Now you have to pay extra." Her face looked haggard, cruel. The room was stuffy and humid from the bath. I noticed it had no windows. I needed some fresh air.

"How much extra?" I asked after a while, and she told me and I stood up and put on my uniform and gave her the money and walked down the stairs into the hot, sticky night. Then I went back to my ship.

The next day I stayed aboard ship and wrote letters. That night Lars came back, drunk, and found me in my office. He had finally managed some real action with Lonnie, he said. Also, Suzie was asking about me. She made him promise to bring me to see her the following day, our last day in port.

So after lunch we went back to the Do Re Mi. Suzie was resplendent in purple silk. Over a beer, she asked me a million questions. Why hadn't I been to see her? Didn't I like her? Did I like someone else better? Was I some kind of butterfly, flitting from girl to girl? I could have sworn she knew all about my evening in the hotel. I had the duty, I said, and had to stay on ship. Then I came to see her but she was not here. Her baby was sick. Was her baby truly sick? Where was her baby? Her baby lived outside of town, with some of Mamasan's relatives. Did I think she was lying, was with somebody else? How could I say such a thing? She was my girlfriend; I was her very nice sailor boy. I had been bad, though, had stayed away three whole days, and now my ship was leaving. I would come back, though, next time, and see her, wouldn't I? I would write letters to her? Her dark eyes were absolutely sparkling. She looked so young and pretty and hopeful. We kissed and made up, and I found it hard to keep my hands off the beautiful purple silk.

We all went to see *My Fair Lady* again, and then to the restaurant by the Do Re Mi. There was a Fourth of July dance at the Enlisted Men's Club that night. The girls were very excited about it. Lars and I wanted instead to go back to their apartment. We all agreed to do both.

At the Club, they flitted from table to table, talking to their girlfriends from other bars. Lars and I drank scotch. One of the sonar men joined us.

"Scuttlebutt is," he said, "because of July Fourth anyone who wants to take an overnight can do it, no questions asked." It almost sounded fishy. Overnights were restricted to second class petty officers and above. But I trusted the sonar man, and Lars and I decided to do it. If we *were* called on the carpet, the punishment wouldn't be too bad, probably just restriction when we arrived up at Keelung, near Taipei.

The girls joined us again, wanting to dance, which we did. Then we left, after buying a bottle of scotch. When we arrived at the apartment, we all drank scotch and water without ice, and I told the girls we could stay the night. It was hot in the kitchen, and Lars and I stripped down to our skivvies. Lonnie put on a kimono, and Suzie changed into a shortie nightgown like girls back in the States wore to slumber parties. I looked down into the alley for the rat, but it wasn't there.

"Give me a cigarette," Lars said. I picked up my shirt and reached into the pocket.

"Damn, there's only one left!"

"Lonnie, do you or Suzie have any?" Lars asked.

"Sorry 'bout that, Songbird."

So Lars and I flipped a coin and he lost. He put his uniform back on and went out into the night to see what he could find.

"Why you smoke, anyway?" Lonnie asked me.

"Well..., because I like it, I guess. Sometimes it helps me think, or helps me stay awake."

"How long you smoke?"

"I smoked some when I was in junior high, to act big. But I really started about five years ago."

"What is junior high?"

"School. Like when you're about twelve years old."

"Cigarettes bad for you," Lonnie said. "Make you smell bad. Not good for you here." She put her hands on her breasts and pushed in. "What's it called?"

"Tits?"

"You dumb puke head! Inside!"

"Lungs?"

"Yeah, lungs. Cigarette very bad for lungs. Make you die."

She reached for the bottle of scotch and poured herself some more. "What about that scotch?" I asked. "Is that bad for you too?"

"No, no, whisky fine. Make you feel good. Make you forget. You think you big damn man, you fuck long time, make Chinese girl happy." She pronounced it "hoppy." "But cigarette very bad. You wait, you see. Someday soon you quit."

Lars came back with a couple of packs of some atrocious Chinese cigarette and we had a few more drinks and then drifted off to the bedrooms.

To make a long story short, I spent the night with Suzie but never got anywhere. Oh, I tried. We kissed and petted, but like virtue incarnate she kept her legs crossed and my balls got to aching something fierce, and she poured the scotch down me until I decided I would probably rather sleep anyway. She made me promise again and again to write letters to her, and to come back to Kaohsiung to see her. I fell asleep sometime after three, and the alarm went off at half past five.

The girls insisted on going back to the pier with us. Then, they said, they would go over to the battlements at the mouth of the harbor and wave to us as the ship left port. I paid the taxi driver and we all got out of the cab and Suzie kissed me and held me tight and said good-bye, good-bye again, and then Lars and I took the shuttle back to the ship. I was still drunk and a little afraid that we might be written up for an unauthorized overnight, but we went on board and saluted the Flag, and saluted the Officer of the Deck, and nothing happened.

I gulped a quick cup of coffee before the special sea and anchor detail was called, then went up to my lookout post, and soon we were underway. As we cleared the harbor, we saw Suzie and Lonnie and a few other girls on the walls, waving at the ship. Suzie was looking straight ahead. I had expected her eyes to be searching for me. She probably figured she wouldn't be able to pick me out anyway. Maybe she needed glasses. I waved to her, and called, but she didn't raise her eyes above the main deck, and never saw me.

After the detail was secured, I went down to my locker to change from my tropical whites into my work clothes. It was then that I discovered my wallet was missing.

We spent four or five days patrolling the Straits of Formosa, eavesdropping on the Red Chinese, and single-handedly preventing them from invading Taiwan. Then, we steamed into Keelung, a busy northern harbor near Taipei.

The loss of my wallet, or rather the loss of my Navy I.D. and liberty card, meant automatic restriction to the ship for the week, so I was unable to go ashore in Keelung. I had good company, though. Lars was also restricted to the ship. Lonnie had given him a dose of the clap.

We spent our torpid evenings sitting in folding chairs up on the flying bridge, smoking cigarettes, watching the lights twinkle on moored ships and the surrounding hills, and holding long, delightfully upset conversations about the human condition.

Six

Heading back toward Vietnam, the Captain decided to hold speed trials. I can't remember the exact rationale for these exercises, but they involve running the ship at full steam for six or seven hours and trying to maintain top speed, which in our case was about twenty-eight knots. It is an unpleasant experience. The noise and vibration increase considerably, and the poor devils in the boiler rooms are subjected to temperatures close to 120 degrees.

About ten-thirty that night, Young, the stuttering fireman, asked permission to go topside for a break. It was denied. Fifteen minutes later he asked again, saying he was so hot he thought he would become sick, and he was told to be back in ten minutes. When after thirty minutes he hadn't returned, the Chief Boilerman sent someone to look for him. "Look in his bunk first," he said. "That's where the son of a bitch was the last time he skipped out on a watch." The crewman couldn't find him. The speed trials were completed shortly before midnight, and when the Chief went off watch he instructed the duty master-at-arms to search the ship.

At two a.m. they woke the Captain and reported that Young appeared to be missing. He was last seen a little before eleven, topside, fumbling with a pack of cigarettes and heading for the fantail. The Captain ordered the ship to reverse course and return to its eleven o'clock position. He also ordered another search of the entire ship, including all of the locked compartments. He radioed a call for assistance, which was answered by another destroyer and a merchant ship. We reached the general area at dawn and were joined by search planes from the Philippines. The special sea and anchor detail was set, and every few yards along the rail an extra lookout was posted.

There are standard procedures you follow in these cases, and standard navigational patterns. We steamed slowly, and made a continual series of right angle turns, forming a pattern of interlocking rectangles about two miles on the long side. It was hot. The calm surface of the sea revealed nothing. From time to time one of the search planes flew low overhead. Up on the flying bridge, we had the slightest of breezes. For two directions of the rectangle it was all right; for the other two, the smoke and heat from the stacks floated down to enfold and suffocate us. The same thing would happen on hot harvest days when I was a kid, spending the summer on my uncle's farm in Kansas. I would stand up on the old tractor-pulled combine, controlling the height of the cutting bar. I had to stand right in front of the combine's engine. For two directions around the wheat field the breeze was with you. The other two directions it blew the engine's baking heat right through you, and it was murder.

The odds for Young weren't good. He must have been in the water all night, without a life jacket. Speculation among the crew was rife.

"That fucker probably jumped, man. He never did have his full ration of brains."

"Nah, man, he just keeled over the fucking rail. You know how fucking hot it was down in the boiler room?"

"I bet he's hid in some compartment somewhere and now he's too scared to come out."

"He was fucking blind in Keelung, man. I seen him one night and he was wasted."

"Wait, what if somebody pushed him? You ever think about that? There's some weird dudes on this tin can."

Just before supper we secured from the search and resumed course for Vietnam. The loudspeaker gave its preparatory little whistle. "This is the Captain speaking." He read a prayer out of a little book for such occasions. We asked especially for the Eternal Commodore to comfort Fireman

Young's parents in their hour of suffering. And just what, I wondered, was the telegram from the Chief of Naval Personnel going to tell them? There were guys in the Pentagon who wrote dozens of these things every day now. Maybe the ambiguity of this one would be a challenge, would make somebody's morning. "I deeply regret to inform you that your son..." Would it tell his parents that in my own way I am praying for them now, and for their lost, lost boy?

For the next thirty days we were assigned to IV Corps, the southernmost war zone. We had a heavy, exhausting schedule of bombardment, and fired several thousand rounds. Once, rumor had it, we were in hot water because we overshot a target and wasted some South Vietnamese troops.

We spent many days in the Mekong Delta, and at night when not firing would head back to the open water near Vung Tau for safety. Dozens of merchant marine vessels were moored there, waiting their turn to go upriver to Saigon and unload the Great Society. They were dazzlingly lit at night, as were the small junks and bumboats that hovered there, and the place looked like a carnival. At dawn, you would see peasant families squatting in the little boats, eating breakfast. It was probably safer than spending the night ashore.

Sometimes the Captain and a few of the officers would go into Vung Tau for briefings. They always had a few cocktails there and would come back with determined warrior faces. The crew was tired, tired, tired. Moving so much ammunition, there was always a chance someone would drop a round in one of the magazines and blow us all to pieces. In the Delta, we fired a lot of three-inch shells because we were closer to the targets. I got to wondering what would happen if one of the shells I loaded exploded in the gun. I would be dead before I even heard the sound, Josephs said.

Seven

The jungle surrounded me with its profusion of growth, its strong moist smell of decay. I walked the few feet back to the manicured lawn and looked up at the mansion, sitting in colonial splendor somewhere on the vast holdings of the base at Subic. It had been converted into an Enlisted Men's Club, and Lars and I had been spending a pleasant afternoon drinking gin on the screened veranda. The wind was rising steadily, and the tall trees swayed like masts against the darkening sky.

A Filipino waiter in starched white linen came out to the end of the lawn to tell us that a typhoon warning had been posted. All personnel attached to ships were ordered to return and prepare to get underway. We went back inside and ordered another drink.

"Typhoon warning?" Lars asked. "Did you hear a typhoon warning?"

"Not me, Sir," I answered. "I was takin' a long walk in the jungle, lookin' for Huks. I never heard nothin' about no typhoon." A while later, the manager came around to repeat the orders about returning to ships.

"We're on temporary shore duty," Lars told him.

"Yeah," I said, "just waiting to get flown back to the states."

We drank for another hour and watched the rain begin to slash across the manicured lawn. You could see the jungle creeping, an inch at a time, to engulf the hedges and the sidewalks and starched linen, to make a fine leafy ruin of the American Century.

They closed the club early, and a last shuttle took us down to the main base. Where that morning there had been

57

seven or eight destroyers, there were now only empty docks, with rain drops making hypnotic patterns on the oil slicked puddles of the pier.

"Of all the nerve," one of us said. "To leave without even saying good-bye."

"Maybe the storm will take her down to Davey Jones."

"Then they'll reassign us to shore duty in Honolulu or San Francisco."

"Or to one of those swift boats that boards junks."

We stood out of the wind under a covered bus stop with some other fugitives, smoking and joking until a van picked us up and took us to a barracks where we were processed in and given supper. I was drinking coffee, beginning to sober up, when I saw Mr. Hooper walk in the door, dressed in foul weather gear and dripping wet.

"If anyone here is from the Buckett," he yelled, "report to me!" We tried to scrunch down, but he saw us and beckoned.

"Captain's compliments," he said, when we were gathered together. "You ready for a fun boat ride?"

A few hours after we returned to the ship, the typhoon hit full force, with winds between eighty and ninety miles an hour. We were in the bay, with both anchors out, and were making steam for eight knots just to stay in place. Two special watches were set, which relieved each other every two hours. It was ridiculous. Half the ship had to stand these watches; the other half could loll around and sleep or watch movies, while we wore ourselves out. Jefferson and I had to hang on to the rail for dear life just to stand at our places on the flying bridge. The rain drove into our faces like nails, and we couldn't see two feet in front of us. We wore foul weather gear, but were soaked to the skin within two minutes.

"Lookout to Bridge. We can't see a thing up here. It's too dark and it's raining too hard."

"Bridge to lookouts. Stay at your posts. Keep a sharp eye out." It was Brock.

"But it's impossible to see a damned thing up here, sir. Request permission to stand our watch down in the wheelhouse."

"Bridge to lookouts. Stay at your posts, keep a sharp watch. That's an order."

We stood there about ten more minutes, and then groped to the rear of the auxiliary wheelhouse, out of the wind, and hunched down on the gear locker. At midnight we were relieved, but were back on watch at two a.m., then six, etc. Whenever we started a watch, we would stand there for five minutes, inform Ensign Brock that it was still impossible to see a thing, and then retire to our sheltered spot.

Jefferson and I had lots of time to talk. We dreamed up the Typhoon Goddess, who could whoosh around the world and bring us news of what our loved ones were doing that very moment. He learned more about me than I would normally have revealed. I learned a great deal about his mother and father, brothers and sisters, cousins, girlfriends, and buddies on the streets of Denver. That afternoon, he had worked his way so far into the labyrinths of his soul that he told me this....

"When we was in Honolulu, see, me and Smitty and Taylor was drunk in this bar. Weren't no other swabbies in there at all. This one cat he takes us back to his place and gives us more booze and says he really wants to suck us off. I didn't want him to do it but Taylor he's saying come on man, he done me. Dig it. Get your nose opened. So I let him. Then we took all the dude's money and split. Uh... sometimes I'm really worried, man."

"What about?"

"Like, what if I got to fill out some forms for a job, or something, and they ask me..."

"Forget it. Pretend it never happened."

"But what if I got to take a lie detector test or something? What if..."

"Bridge to lookouts," Brock suddenly boomed out over our headphones, "why didn't you report that barge that just

59

crossed our bow?" We jumped up and peered over the sides, but couldn't see a thing.

"Lookout to bridge. I'll report once again that it's impossible for us to see anything up here."

"Well, a runaway barge just came within about ten feet of smashing into the ship. If it had hit us, your asses would have been mud."

"Even if we can't see anything?"

"That's right, sailors. Somebody would have to take the rap and it sure as shit wouldn't be me." Thanks, Brock.

"You think this wind is ever gonna stop?" Jefferson asked me.

"I don't know. Let's ask the Typhoon Goddess."

The Typhoon Goddess tells us sure, sailor boys, you'll be out of this in no time, so Jefferson and I crouch down and relax. He closes his eyes and I whisper to the Typhoon Goddess, "Yeah, but what happens when this is all over?"

She laughs and punches me lightly in the stomach.

"Lover boy," she says, "no way can I tell you twisty turns you take next ten, twenty years. Next two three months mebbe yes. You get back stateside, buy car. America it Craazy. You move in my Songbird's house. His Mamasan one fine woman, you love her like mother.

"You drive San Francisco. You say you no fuck that girl you no love, but you fuck her anyway. Girl you do love she only talk poems with you, she no love you, she alla time busy. Sorry 'bout that. You go back San Diego. Officer boss man he say you too short time, you be transfer off ship. You think they send you back Vietnam but you get one big surprise, they send you type type big building. You not on ship you one lucky sailor.

"You ride ship one last time, back San Francisco. Girl you love she blonde, she pretty, she curious. She want visit you ship. You put on uniform, you and my Songbird, you take her there. Alla sailor boys they jealous, she one damn broad, she officer woman. You take her round, show her office, mess hall, tip top part of ship here. My Songbird he talk too much, he say you load big bullets in gun, he say ship kill seven hunnerd VC, if you believe way officer boss men count. He talk too much, he piss you off, you sad. You go back brother's house, you stop buy Irish Whiskey. Girl you love she drink just one drink then go. She butterfly maybe. You walk to her car. She have to tell you something. When she look you in eyes she see you not same as before. Something fly away, dead maybe. She worry for you. She kiss you on cheek. She drive away. You write her one letter, she write you one letter, you never see her again. Never."

That evening, the storm began to subside. The special watches were relieved, and I slept ten hours straight. The next afternoon we went back in and tied up at the pier. All hands, however, were restricted to base. There was two feet of water in the streets of Olongapo and, supposedly, cholera. The crews complained bitterly. The EM clubs on the base were full every night. The mood was surly, and there were several fistfights. What was life without Olongapo whores? I would have gone over too, if I could.

Before the restriction was lifted, the Buckett got underway for Vietnam again. Only twelve days on the line, then home, via Japan.

Only two days left. We were in II Corps, off a free fire zone. Someone somewhere had decided that people in a free fire zone were assumed to be hostile. Whether they told that to the people I don't know.

We cruised about a thousand yards offshore, awaiting orders. I was on watch, and a beautiful sunset was beginning to happen. The hills were turning from green to dark blue, and the heavens behind were purple and turquoise and golden.

"Bridge to port lookout. How do you make the structure onshore, bearing 300 degrees?" It was easy to spot, being the only building visible on the bluffs. I had already been looking at it through binoculars, watching its walls turn pink in the sunset.

"Port lookout to bridge. I'd say it's a Buddhist temple or monastery, Sir. It has one of those pagodas with rings on it."

"Do you see any activity around there, Feldkirchen?"

"No, Sir, none at all."

A few minutes later the ship's speaker buzzed into life. "Mount 51 will commence firing in two minutes. All hands stand clear of the forward gun platform." The mount below me began to swivel around in its twitchy fashion, and I could see that it was being locked on to the temple.

One round was fired. I saw no sign of an explosion or hit. I looked over the side of the flying bridge and saw the Captain, the Executive Officer, and Mr. Skelton standing on the wing below me. The Captain was wearing his khaki shorts and the Australian Ranger hat he had been given in Vung Tau. They all had binoculars trained on the temple. The Captain turned and yelled into the wheelhouse. "Fire three more rounds!"

One. Two. Three. There was a puff of smoke and dust as one of the rounds hit the wall to the left of the pagoda. The three officers cheered. It was as if they were at a football game. "You've got the range," the Captain shouted. "I want that tower!" It took seven more rounds for it to crumble.

They were grinning, and slapping each other on the back. I almost couldn't blame them. For five months they had been out here. They'd fired over ten thousand rounds, but never once had they damned the torpedoes, full speeded ahead, or seen the whites of any eyes. Never had they watched a shell tear into something or blow it apart. Never once had anyone shot back at us. What were we, a bunch of chicken shits? No, dammit, here at last we had made our war. Finally, something had happened.

However, we were still bloody idiots, and criminals to boot. Summary Court Martial for unauthorized bombardment? But who was there to judge us? Then I saw him, descending toward us about fifteen hundred yards off the starboard bow. It was the Avenging Angel of the Lord, and with one stroke of his gleaming sword he smote the Buckett exactly in twain. The sparks from metal on metal found a newly exposed ammo magazine, and a series of explosions sent fragments of iron and remnants of people spiraling to the ocean floor. Then all was quiet, and there was nothing to be seen on the surface of the sea but shimmering reflections of the sunset. A gong began to sound in the miraculously restored pagoda, calling the tranquil, holy monks to prayer.

Our last day on the firing line. One of the aft five-inch guns let fly a few from time to time. A destroyer was approaching, and word passed quickly through the ship that our relief was here. The crew began to line the rails, to have a look at her. She was older than the Buckett, with a slightly different type of five-inch gun. Through binoculars, we could see that she was at general quarters. All topside personnel were wearing flak jackets and metal helmets.

"This is the Captain speaking. We're heading for Japan. Secure from Condition III, set Condition IV. Let's start getting this ship ready for stateside." A scattered cheer went up, and we began to increase speed. So it was back to spit and polish already. As the coast receded, we saw that the other destroyer had already begun to fire.

I went down to the fantail and watched Vietnam disappear. I was too tired to feel much of anything. It was over, that was all. I headed for my office, stretched out on the steel floor, and fell asleep.

Eight

I asked for, and was granted, three days of leave in Japan. I changed into my suit at the Yokosuka train station and went up to Tokyo, where I caught the bullet train to Kyoto. I went to one of the new hotels, across from the old Imperial Palace. From my window, I could look down and watch the rain sweep across the red tiled roofs of the city, and look at the fog-wisped hills beyond. I took a bath and slept until supper.

It was a Time of Revelations, and the first one arrived when I went up to the top floor restaurant. I was walking along the corridor, lost in the ornate pattern of the rug. I saw a pair of tennis shoes and my gaze moved up, and up, to meet that of the first white woman I had seen in five months. My God, she was six feet tall! She could have played fullback for Penn State! I'm sure my jaw dropped open, for she gave me a confused look and hurried past.

Revelation number two arrived the next morning at breakfast. I sat at a small table, reading the *New York Times*. My coffee arrived in a delicate china cup and I absentmindedly took a sip. I almost fell out of my chair. For six months I had been drinking whatever that shipboard slop was, but it certainly wasn't coffee.

That day, I went on an extensive bus tour of the city and its environs. The following morning I took a taxi up to a Zen shrine in the hills that had been my favorite spot the day before. There was a light rain and the grounds were deserted. I sat in a small covered shelter, looking at the sand garden and the carefully tended shrubs and the city down on the plain.

I tried to absorb it all, the peace and the beauty, and tried to call forth those quasi-spiritual feelings I had known before enlisting and had cultivated in boot camp. For some reason, I kept thinking of Julian of Norwich, five hundred years ago holding an acorn in her hand and seeing in it the entire universe. I picked up a small rock and gazed at it, but it was just a small rock, and whatever it was in which I lived and moved and had my being had grown crooked and stale. I couldn't even cry.

I took the fast train back to Tokyo, and wandered about the clogged streets. I looked in the windows of pachinko parlors and couldn't tell the people from the machines. I went into an underground shopping mall and became lost in its mazes. I found a quiet little subterranean bar and drank Suntory whisky. I went back up into the crowded streets and entered a restaurant with molded plastic reproductions of all the menu items in the window. I brought the waitress out onto the sidewalk and pointed out to her the meal I wanted.

I arrived in Yokosuka at eleven p.m., but I didn't want to go back to the ship until the next morning when I absolutely had to. So I asked the taxi driver to take me to a hotel. We drove to a large squat building on a winding road above the town. Its clientele were sailors and their bar girls. The place was noisy and I slept fitfully. At five-thirty my wake-up call came, and I ordered a taxi. I dressed in my uniform and opened the window to look at the lovely morning. There, lying on a ledge two or three feet below the sill, was a used condom. Goodbye, Asia.

Everything happened the way the Typhoon Goddess said it would. Back in the States I bought a green '61 Volvo. My father paid for half of it. I moved into Sondberg's home in San Diego and grew fondly dependent on his mother's wisdom.

I took two weeks of leave and went to San Francisco. I had resolved to break off with Mary, but didn't. I couldn't bring myself to tell her she was just a form of therapy. While she was at work I went to bookstores and bars and visited friends. I only saw Miranda once, as she was busy with graduate school and a great deal of socializing. One afternoon we sat on her patio in the hills and drank Irish Whiskey while she described the research she was doing about Yeats. She asked me what I wanted to do when I got out of the Navy, and I had no idea. I just wanted out.

I also visited with my brother. While I was in WESTPAC, he and his wife had moved from Long Beach to San Francisco. He was going to law school, and had a poster of Che Guevara in his living room.

When I returned to my ship, I heard a few things the Typhoon Goddess had forgotten to mention. The Captain had been promoted, and was about to transfer to the War College for advanced leadership training. Good job, well done.

Pedrelli, the fellow I had spent so many long, quiet hours with on the flying bridge, was in jail. From a bar somewhere in San Diego, he had been lured to a motel room by a man who then made advances. Pedrelli had stabbed him and he died. Pedrelli claimed self-defense, but the cops asked why, if it were self- defense, had he stabbed the victim seventeen times?

The Executive Officer called me to his office. "You've heard about this short timer rotation order, Feldkirchen?"

"Yes, Sir."

"You're not exactly a short timer, but when your enlistment is up, the Buckett will be back in WESTPAC. The Navy is trying to save travel money."

"I know, Sir."

"Normally, you'd be transferred to a ship leaving for Vietnam soon, but I have a message here from COMCRUDESPAC," by which he meant the Commander of the Cruiser-Destroyer Force of the Pacific Fleet. "The Admiral needs yeomen on his staff. That would mean shore duty here in San Diego. He only wants dedicated sailors, good typists. Now you proved yourself pretty well in WESTPAC, Feldkirchen, but I haven't forgotten that AWOL incident. If I recommend you for this duty, you'll have to promise me you won't fuck up."

"I won't fuck up, Sir."

"Watch your language, sailor."

"Sorry, Sir."

"You'll have to keep on your toes on the Admiral's staff, Feldkirchen."

"Yes, Sir."

"All right, I'll see what I can do, but you'd better not let me down."

"No, Sir. One thing, Sir."

"Yes?"

"Is it true we're headed for San Francisco in a few weeks?"

"That's right. The whole flotilla. I'm looking forward to it. The maneuvers are timed to have us there for the Stanford-Navy game." So much for saving on travel money.

"Sir, will I be transferred before or after we go to San Francisco?"

"After. Dismissed."

I saluted and left, and walked up to the flying bridge to look around. I could see the building that housed the Admiral's staff. I had carried reports there from time to time. It would be easy duty, but I would be bored silly.

I lit a cigarette and looked down at the main deck. Clyde and some others were chipping the paint off the outside of Mount 51. I wouldn't miss that gun. But I would miss the incredibly deep blue of mid-ocean, the sunsets, and the crazy patterns of the staked fishing nets along the Vietnamese coast. I would miss quiet temples, and the bustle and smells of a sweltering Asian street. And I would never see the Typhoon Goddess again. One hand giveth, the other taketh away. Part of me almost wanted to go back.

BROTHER ANDREW

One

God, lustrous God, was behind it all, and God worked in strange ways. Truly. Like yesterday, when Chris entered that office and one of the little cards on the opposite wall, on the job board, began to glow and pulsate the way the whole sterile room would have were he on LSD. God marked that job, and Chris trusted.

Oh, he knew that the Wondrous Mind was magnitudes greater than galaxies, let alone this wretched planet or his utterly foolish person. Even so, some autonomous, minute aspect of that Glory must be controlling these events, leading him to his Ultimate Destiny. And he wanted that . . . that Spiraling Thing to realize that he knew that it knew that he ...

And the Children of Light! And Brother Andrew! The little poster announcing the lecture, stuck on that pole on Woodside Road where no one ever put posters, had been placed there just for him. He caught a glimpse of the beard, the smile, the old-fashioned broad brimmed hat, and simply had to pull Old Ford to the side of the road, walk back, and take a good look.

"God is Everywhere," the poster said, "and God is Bliss, and the Bliss is You." And this man, Brother Andrew, looking no older than Chris, beamed out at him like the keeper of the secret keys.

He went to the lecture, down at Foothill Junior College, in the same room where his film theory class had been held that spring. About two dozen others had also answered the call. Brother Andrew came in, with two or three . . . . what were they . . . friends, followers, disciples? Lifting slightly the white folds of his monkish robe, he seated himself on the top of the desk and glowed for about ten minutes. His companions began to vibrate with that glow, and Chris could see how very . . . There . . . they must feel. Soon that light, that joy just filled the room. Wave after wave kept emanating from the man. Chris soaked it in; it filled every empty space he had ever had. Then Brother Andrew spoke, and he spoke in the purest King's English, and that clinched it.

"It's such a lovely autumn day. Shall we adjourn outside?"

So they all went out, found a quiet spot of lawn behind the building, and sat there in the sun for a few moments before Brother Andrew spoke again.

"A blind man came to Jesus to be healed. Jesus picked up a handful of dirt, spit on it, and made two little balls of mud to put on the blind man's eyes. When He removed the mud He asked 'what do you see?' The patient said 'I see men as trees walking,' and Jesus said 'Hmmm,' picked up some more dirt, spit on it, and again rubbed it into the man's eyes. This time He had it right. Now what does this say to you?"

Brother Andrew paused for a while, then continued. "Is it possible that there has been a fundamental mistake, that we all have had only the first half of the treatment, and see not clearly? I say it is not only possible, but tragically true. I shan't enter the argument whether God or humanity is to blame. The cure, the Light, is everywhere, but those who truly see are few. My message is simple. Seek and ye shall find."

Chris knew that nothing original had been said, but he was utterly shaken. The words had been just for him! And the way the man spoke, and looked, and made him feel! Brother Andrew nodded to one of the women with him. High as a kite, Chris thought. Beautiful. About nineteen, long brown hair, eyes like green water; a pre-Raphaelite goddess. Her radiance made him want to cry.

"Brother Andrew," she said, "is in our country to establish centers for the Children of Light, a world-wide organization headquartered in Switzerland. The Children of Light are followers of all religions, and of no religion but the

Prayer of the Heart. This is a simple technique that can lead you to the Bliss within. Brother Andrew charges no fees to teach this technique. The Bliss of God should be as free to all as air and water. Brother Andrew has taken vows of poverty and chastity, and has few needs."

She named the address in Palo Alto where he could be found and invited everyone to attend their morning gatherings to be instructed in the Prayer of the Heart. Brother Andrew and his people stood up, made some ritual farewells. Chris watched as all that holiness walked shimmering away across the green lawn, and suddenly (odd, wasn't it?) into his head popped the thought that as long as he was on campus he might as well check the job board.

He stood there, in the door, as the three by five card winked at him. It had become so simple, he thought, this path to wherever he was being led. Peeling away outer layers until nothing is left, then losing that also. And then what? He saw that even the mistakes, the pain, had served to propel him through this door to whatever would . . . .

He walked over to the card and read it. Subscription clerk, half time, for a graphic arts magazine. Perfect! He sat down to wait his turn. Mrs. Wells was talking to a jock, short hair, all muscle. Six foot four, maybe, two-twenty-five, wearing a jersey with a big number 69 on the back. Of course! Who that size ever thinks about God, or sainthood, or giving up the world? They *own* the fucking world, the poor devils. How absurd he had been ever to pity himself for being a skinny weakling. All part of the plan!

The jock left and Chris moved over to the empty chair, which still held the warmth of those burning, carnivorous calories.

"Hello, Mrs. Wells."

"Hi," she said, and asked herself "Ken, Kurt?" She reached for her cigarette, burning in the ashtray, and he felt so much compassion for her, this familiar, anxious matron with permed orange hair and too much makeup. A slightly

73

twitching hand, fueled by self-destruction, brought the cigarette to her lips.

Now she remembered. Chris. Chris some funny German something. For he in turn was familiar to her. Tall, thin, with hair down past his neck. Not much chin, too much ear, but nice nose and eyes. A drooping moustache, an intense, rapt expression. Always wearing the same old clothes: battered hush puppies, tan Levi's, a shapeless brown sweater over a work shirt with a frayed collar. Polite, soft spoken, a little pretentious. A Vietnam veteran, a bit older than most of the other junior college students. Graduated in June, in spite of all that Kent State mess, but still coming in to use her job service. The poor guy.

Chris knew she must be tired of him, after five or six months. He doesn't seem in any real hurry to find a job, she probably says. Who the hell does he think he is? Who indeed?

"Uh, can I help you, Chris?"

"Yes, please. I'm interested in the subscription clerk position."

She reached into her drawer for his file. "Uh . . . what was your last name again, Chris?"

"Feldkirchen."

"Oh, yes, silly of me."

She phoned to arrange an interview, then filled out a card for him to take. The magazine had its offices in Palo Alto, on California Avenue. So that was it! Only two blocks from the Children of Light! She made some notes in his file, then looked up and smiled.

"Good luck," she said. "Uh, perhaps you should go home and change before the interview."

Change! Dear God, change! If she had the slightest idea of the changes he'd been through her brains would melt down into butter.

"You know," she said, "wear a tie or something." He didn't even have a tie, only two other work shirts, another pair of tan Levi's, and an old winter coat from a thrift store.

"I'll give it my best, Mrs. Wells. Thanks."

74

An hour later he was there. He took one of those tests which tell if you can read and remember a series of numbers and letters. The Office Manager, Mrs. Presto, expressed amazement at his speed and accuracy. She was more or less a carbon copy of Mrs. Wells, except that her hair was blue rather than orange, and instead of Winstons she smoked Newports. She lit one, and showed him the magazine: slick, expensive, oriented toward advertising art. She walked him down the hall to a little room with no windows, and ran through the duties.

There was this perfectly marvelous chrome-handled tool that looked like a hole punch. Place a letter in the slot, push down the handle, and clean as a guillotine the top sliver of the envelope is sliced off. Remove the contents. Stamp the check on the back with the rubber endorsement stamp. If the stamp pad needs to be re-inked, the ink is in the bottom desk drawer. When all the checks are stamped, add them up on the old cranker and fill out a deposit slip. Then walk to the bank and make the deposit. Afterward, give the verified copy of the slip to the bookkeeper.

Divide all the subscription forms into new and renewals, then put each pile in alphabetical order. For new subscriptions, make out a three by five card like that one no longer winking in Mrs. Wells' office, and put all the relevant information on it. Then make an addressograph master. For a renewal, update the existing card. Make a new addressograph master for renewals, too, as there is no way to alter the date on the old ones. Once a month run off an entire set of labels and give them to the mailing crew. Also once a month send out a renewal form to those whose subscriptions are about to expire.

If you are living in the Light, Feldkirchen knows, the job is like a form of prayer. Not attached to the work, you neither love nor hate it, but focus on the repetition, as with a mantra or rosary, and offer the work to God. The result is inner peace and enough of a paycheck each month to satisfy your simple needs.

The lesson over, they walked back to the main office and Mrs. Presto lit another cigarette. She looked at him forcefully.

"I'm not sure," she said. "You don't seem like the kind of person who would want this job. Wouldn't you be bored with it?"

"Oh, no, not at all."

"The girl who just quit said it was too lonely in that little office."

"Loneliness is not a problem for me."

"It's a real bother if people quit after a few months, having to train somebody new and all."

"No, this job would be perfect. I'm sure the morning would just fly by."

Her eyes turned to surprise. "Morning? Don't you have classes at Foothill in the mornings?"

"No, I graduated in June." The surprise turned to suspicion. "In Communications," he added meaningfully.

"You expect to make a living on this salary?" she asked.

It was touch and go. But then he saw it happen. God pushed a button somewhere, in her head or up in Command Central, and her face just changed, the suspicion and anxiety turning to a sort of vague wonder.

"Really," he said, "the job is just great. When would you like me to start?"

"To start? Oh . . . .uh, what's today? Thursday?"

"Yes, Thursday. Shall I start tomorrow?"

"Well," she said, crushing her cigarette out in a bean bag ashtray, "why don't you start Monday?"

On the drive up to Skyline, he prayed Old Ford would make it to work and back every day. She was a '54 Mainliner, faded green, four doors, cheap new upholstery. Every seventy-five miles or so he had to clean the spark plugs and put in a can of STP. Even then she made too much smoke. He'd bought her for a hundred dollars when his Volvo died.

Bob, Nancy, and the baby weren't home. He made a sandwich and tea, went out to the deck, and sat there while the sun dropped behind the redwoods. He didn't use the deck so much now that he shared the house and had moved from the master bedroom down to the little converted workshop. One more layer gone, he thought, and a good exercise in humility. He basked in the Bliss and the fading sunlight. Tomorrow, he knew, he would go down to Brother Andrew and join the Children of Light.

He arrived bright and early at the small Spanish style house a few blocks off California. The young woman with long brown hair opened the door. She introduced herself as Sarah, and asked him to leave his shoes on the porch. In the living room, the stereo played Gregorian chant. Round Zen pillows littered the floor, some form of incense burned, and he noted with a smile the *de rigueur* flowered Indian bedspread tacked on the wall behind the sofa. In the dining room sat the man and other woman who had been with Brother Andrew at the lecture. They had not spoken then, and merely smiled at him now. Perhaps they had reached a stage in the path where speech was pointless. Between them in a high chair sat a fussing baby girl. Brother Andrew sat at the table too, with his white robe, beaming smile, rimless glasses, curly black hair and beard. He nodded, made a little motion with his hand for Chris to sit down, and asked Sarah to serve them tea. It was in large plain mugs, and tasted mostly of milk and honey. Brother Andrew asked his name, and he told him.

"Ah," he said, still beaming. "Sprechen Sie Deutsch, Christoph?"

"No, I don't."

"There was a Feldkirchen at Cambridge when I was there, from Hessen or some such place. He looked rather like you, in fact. Maybe you are distant cousins."

Chris didn't know if this qualified as flattery, or coincidence, or idle chatter, but it was not what was really going on anyway. What was going on was that he sat looking at Brother Andrew's hand, the one that had made the little motion to sit down. An aura of white light danced around each finger, and Chris had a feeling in the top of his head that made him want to close his eyes and dissolve.

Others began to arrive, and settle in the living room. Brother Andrew moved to the sofa. Chris sat on the floor at the rear of the room and watched the flowered bedspread begin to slightly blossom. Then, eyes closed, he had no idea how long he was poised there, the bliss thick enough to stick to his socks. Later, when Brother Andrew began to speak, he realized the Gregorian chants had ended long before.

"Ask yourself," that immaculate Oxbridge voice intoned, "why it is that everyone in the world can't feel the simple joy we feel this morning."

They sat there, asking themselves, and one young woman began to cry softly. Chris didn't have any answers. He didn't, for once, even have any questions. Whatever was, or had been, or would be, was perfect enough.

Brother Andrew stood up, clasped his hands at his chest, Indian style, and went back into one of the bedrooms. When Sarah asked if anyone wanted instruction in the Prayer, three or four besides Chris raised their hands. Sarah gave him a pamphlet that took five minutes to read, about the Prayer of the Heart, the Children of Light, and Father Sergius in Geneva. There were some simple rules of diet, honesty, and clean living. The organization had been formed to do good in the world.

At his turn, he entered the room to find Brother Andrew sitting cross legged on the bed. He sat likewise, facing the white robed saint, who after a few moments asked him "Are you certain this is for you?"

He knew he was finally doing something right in his life, nodded, and Brother Andrew taught him his particular Prayer of the Heart, instructing him not to reveal it to anyone.

As Chris was leaving the room, Brother Andrew crossed to a desk and picked up a spiral notebook, then asked casually, "That was an interesting gadget, wasn't it, the one that slices the tops off envelopes?"

Two

The next day, as he sat by the trickling stream in the forest below his house, it all fell into place. Now he understood. These past few weeks he'd been wallowing in confusion over his recent trip to Canada. Now he knew. God had been saving him for this, for the Children of Light, for Brother Andrew. The Word, he almost dared to think, made Flesh. But why? Where would it lead?

Now he saw why some months earlier God had demolished, for the good of his soul, what was almost beginning to amount to a career. He had been accepted to the Film Institute at San Francisco State, and one afternoon he drove up to look at the production studio. He had been comfortable with his simple super 8 equipment, but now he stood there, surrounded by 16 mm Moviolas and metal chairs, facing a wall full of black panels, buttons, knobs, gauges, and little blinking lights. Something just snapped. It was like Combat Central on his old destroyer, or a place where they bring cats and monkeys to implant electrodes in their brains, perform lobotomies, or conduct malicious experiments with nerve gas.

He should have seen it coming. After Tamiko and he had moved up to Skyline from the Addison Street house, he became more and more reclusive. Then at Christmas, when she moved back down the hill, he turned almost, well, monastic. He went through the motions of going to school but lived his real life here, in the redwoods, with fog and quiet and solitude. In May, when Nixon invaded Cambodia, he didn't strike; he just played hooky. He stayed home all that week and listened as Pacifica Radio unfolded each event, each action, finally Kent State. It all seemed terribly distant, another country. Besides, that wench, the war, for him was long dead.

Now, here he stood, in the metallic soul of where it was at, FILM! . . . and it was blindness, sterility, death. So he simply turned his back on the little twitching arrows and blinking lights, left the studio and drove down Highway One to San Gregorio, where he walked on the beach until dark.

That night after his epiphany at the film lab he smoked a lot of hash, lying out on the deck, looking at the stars. He saw the Milky Way clearly, but it was not the Milky Way. There, hovering above him, blazed the figure of Jesus. "No," said the little stoned voice in his head, "it's just the Milky Way." But he could see perfectly the features of Jesus' face, His flowing hair, His glowing robe and outstretched arms. He could even see the stigmata on those quivering hands and feet. And Jesus was smiling. Lovingly beckoning.

"This is horse shit," he thought. "I'm not a Christian. I'm a Hindu, or a Buddhist . . . or something."

But Jesus still shimmered there, saying "come unto me, all ye who are weary, all ye who thirst..."

Of course! Eastern religion was no more his true, deep down self than film making. He was Greece, and Rome, and Charlemagne and the monasteries and Luther and ...Luther, and Canterbury! And Canterbury, and reading Shelley and Keats in a little rose covered vicarage in Surrey or Sussex; a life of quiet contemplation free of cities, bustle, smog, technology and, and ... EGO!

Jesus twinkled and smiled down on him. He smiled back, and promised to think about it some more, then went in to bed and fell asleep with his two cats curled together in a purring ball next to his feet.

In the morning, he flushed his little stash of dope down the toilet. He had decided to collect wood. He would try not to use the gas furnace at all next winter, but his real motive was purification, not economy. Purification and simplicity. He walked down to the general store at Skylonda Corners and bought a bow saw, one of those little ones with a red tubular handle. No one had cleared the deadfall on the property for years. There was probably tons of it, old redwood mostly, lying this way and that on the steep five acre plot.

He picked branches from the gullies and hillsides, carried them through ferns and oxalis up the hill, and piled them next to the decrepit woodshed by the kitchen door. Usually, he could handle three or four at a time. The occasional large, heavy one he would drag with an end on his shoulder, sweating and straining up the path, trying to imagine the suffering of Jesus bearing the cross through the vile, crowded streets. When he had a good pile he would saw it into lengths and stack it in the shed. Much of the wood was old and rotten and lighter than a feather. Later, he discovered that it made pretty useless firewood. But that was not the point anyway.

In the evenings, exhausted, he would lie in bed with the cats, reading library books on Christianity. In his mind, he vacillated between Catholicism and the Church of England, but was inclined toward the side of Rome. There was something, well, incomplete, cut off, missing about Protestantism. It just didn't have the fullness, the round, all-encompassing two thousand years of the True Church. He found a simple catechism. Its explanation of Apostolic Succession, the Keys of the Kingdom, etc., convinced him. He was struck by the aptness of the metaphors. The Trinity could be thought of in terms of the three states of water: ice, liquid, steam. They were all water, three Gods in One. What really moved him was the soul as balloon. We moderns have flat, empty, airless souls. The sacraments, the Bread and Wine, inflate the balloon, bring our souls back to life, and fill us with grace and joy. He wanted that feeling. For some reason, it never occurred to him to attend church.

Those evenings as he lay there reading, he noticed more and more the noise of the cars and motorcycles going by on Skyline. It had always been the major drawback of this idyllic place, but now it seemed even more intrusive. He had sold his camera and projector and had a little money. When he finished collecting all the deadfall, he decided, it would be time to move to true wilderness.

Then Bob and Nancy were evicted, after their landlord, the one who had made them get rid of their dog, found out about the baby. Chris invited them to move in, to take care of the house and cats. Now he was free to explore.

He spent two days in the library and decided on Nelson, British Columbia. A town in the middle of nowhere, in the mountains. It sheltered a small Catholic college, and it was in Canada. Perhaps he could finally shake the dust of this fascist America from his feet. What he realized now, of course, afterwards, was that his failure lay in trying to plan his own destiny rather than in simply submitting to the marvelous, mysterious, divine will.

He ate a supper of rice and vegetables in a Chinese restaurant in Spokane, and then headed north in the darkness on a small, two lane road. Old Ford, thanks to prayer and the toothbrush he cleaned the spark plugs with, had made it that far. About midnight, a few miles from the border, he pulled into a turnoff and crawled in the back seat to sleep.

In the morning he sat up, in sunshine and in Eden. He had unknowingly parked next to a pasture, with half a dozen horses, palomino and sorrel, nibbling at green grass. A red barn in the distance, the whole scene perfectly framed by rolling hills and blue sky. He was headed, he knew, in the right direction.

He passed customs easily, after showing them his traveler's checks and letting them search the car for firearms. Soon he reached the Canadian Rockies; the vivid yellows and reds of October. He found Nelson a small pleasant town nestled in a valley overlooked by high mountains. He drove around until he wound up at the college. Unimposing, prefabricated, it lacked the tree filled quads or venerable brick buildings he had imagined, but that didn't matter.

He wandered the halls, looking at notices, and stood outside an open door, eavesdropping on a lecture about

Aquinas. He went to the admissions office. The Dean, a small gray haired man with frightened eyes, wore one of those tweed coats with leather elbow patches. He chain smoked, and looked hung over. Chris showed him his transcripts and asked about the possibility of admittance at midyear or the following September.

The Dean stared at the transcripts. They quivered in his slightly shaking hands. "I tell you what," he said. "We're only two weeks into the fall term. I can admit you now, if you like."

Chris was dumfounded. He couldn't believe it. Too good to be true? Well, in fact, yes. A hitch developed. Unmarried, he would have to live in a dorm. He explained that he was twenty-seven years old, a veteran, a vegetarian, and had two cats. He would find it hard to readjust to life at close quarters, to the noise and the meaty, starchy dorm food. He did not want to give up his cats. Was a dispensation possible?

"Maybe," the Dean said. "Let's go talk to the Bursar." But the Bursar was in a meeting. They should come back in an hour.

Now this is the part that troubled him, the part that still went through his mind like a film loop, the part unable to be left on the cutting room floor. He found the chapel, and sat there until his internal frenzy stilled somewhat. "Lord," he prayed, "if I am allowed to enter this college and live off campus, I will become a Catholic, and a good one too. Just please don't ask too great a sacrifice of me yet." If they say yes, he reasoned, that would be his sign; he had found his intended way. Who knows? Perhaps even the priesthood.

He went back to the Dean, and they found the Bursar, a tall bulky Irishman who looked like an ex-football coach. No, the Bursar said, he just couldn't do it. The school had an obligation to protect the immortal souls of its unmarried students. His decision, Chris thought, was probably based on money. But he actually said it. He stood there in his smarmy bulkiness and actually said it. "The school has an obligation to protect the immortal souls of its unmarried students." Chris would have to live in a dorm.

He would think about it, he told them, and let them know in the morning. He went out to Old Ford, and looked at the map. It showed a campground about six miles north of town. He bought a few groceries, and on the way out there picked up a hitch hiker. Spaced out, pretty, long blonde hair, about his age.

"California license plate," she said after a while. "You from the states?"

"Yes."

"You a draft dodger?"

"No, I'm here visiting the college. Maybe I'll go there."

"They're incredibly up tight, eh? A real straight place."

"I'm beginning to understand that."

"Going to college, that keeps you out of the war, eh?"

"It can, yes."

"You Catholic?"

"No."

"You can let me out up by that sign."

He watched her walk up a dirt road. The wind played with strands of her blonde hair, and the sun shone through them, creating a halo. He put the car into gear and drove on to the campground. He took a walk. All of a sudden he grew very lonely. He made a cold supper, and shared it with three squirrels. He stretched out his sleeping bag on a picnic table and crawled inside. He was the only person in the campground. It was dark . . . .

The fucking Catholics. The fucking inflexible, block headed, dogmatic, anti-intellectual, dry rot Catholics.

It grew colder and colder. He got out of the sleeping bag, rolled it up, and put it in the car. He began driving west, and the next morning reached Vancouver. He ate breakfast there, and wondered if the Dean would even remember he had failed to call. The Dean probably didn't care one way or another.

But God cared, Chris realized, as he sat there at home by the trickling stream. God had been leading him around by the nose, trying to teach him a lesson. And God had let him

84

flounder here in near despair for a few weeks before throwing him like a bone to Brother Andrew.

But why? Why ultimately? He wondered if the next little step hadn't been shown him already. After his initiation into the Children of Light he had driven home. Old Ford purred up the hill like a Rolls Royce. Chris made a sandwich and ate on the back lawn, in the sun, then said his Prayer for a long time. He felt jumpy, sweaty, about to burst. He took a shower, and standing there under the stream of hot wet bliss he had the strangest feeling in the base of his spine, as if some sort of giant had awakened from a long sleep, had grown too large for the bed and was stretching its cramped body. Then a voice, not the usual little stoned one, but coming from a slightly different corner of his brain, said "Maybe you should go down to L.A. and help start Children of Light Centers there."

"Whoa," he thought, turning off the shower. "Don't be ridiculous." His least favorite place in the world, the place he had spent his first eighteen years. "Please be just a hallucination," he prayed. "Don't do that one to me God, don't send me to Southern California. Even I don't deserve that!"

When he got out of the shower, the fog had come in and the wind had risen, and it looked like rain.

Three

There is a gathering every weekday morning at seven, and on Wednesday and Saturday evenings. To start, there is angelic music. Then Brother Andrew enters, ever calm, slow, emanating a palpable bliss. All sit in silence for thirty or forty minutes, while the Prayer of the Heart fills the room. Then there are questions. Chris never has questions; all his have been answered. Brother Andrew treats all queries with respect, but the sillier ones cause his eyes to twinkle.

"If we meditate long enough, can we discover our past lives?"

"Yes, but the question then becomes whether or not we want to. If you accept the premise that reincarnation leads us to successively higher stages of being, and ultimately to enlightenment, then our work should be concerned with spiritual advancement and not with trivia, what the Church would call adiaphora, such as whether we were ever in Atlantis or connected to the court of Pharaoh. This is analogous to gaining any powers, what the Hindus call siddhis, such as, say, telekinesis. If you worked diligently enough, following the right methods, you could after several years learn to levitate this cushion across the room. But isn't it so much easier just to use your hands?"

He throws the pillow squarely into the lap of the questioner. Everyone laughs and understands.

"What is death?" another asks.

"Death is unimportant."

Silence, then "Uh . . . why did you take a vow of celibacy? Will you . . . uh, eventually expect us to?"

"I made my vow when I had reached a stage in my spiritual practice where desire could be transmuted to a

86

higher plane, could be transformed into a love energy which is, frankly, more satisfying, more of an intense, lasting bliss than the fumbling, fleeting pleasures of sex. I do not ask anyone to take a vow of celibacy. I ask you only to be moderate, and to practice the Prayer of the Heart, and if the Prayer leads you in the direction of celibacy, then follow the leading that God gives."

"What is the best way to lose weight?"

The twinkle grows in Brother Andrew's eyes. "Practice the Prayer of the Heart. All answers, all changes, flow from that. The answers will come not from me, but from the God within you."

Then he stands up, and with his hands clasped in front of his chest, wishes them farewell, and Sarah brings him the mug of tea which is mostly milk and honey, and he retires to the back room.

People leave, and stand in small clots on the lawn, or lean against their cars. They chatter. Chris tries to ignore the chatter, but can't help overhearing, and sometimes stops to listen. He doesn't know where the rumors come from, or their purpose Most are about Father Sergius in Geneva. He is such a revered master that beings in space ships come to him from other planets to be initiated into the Prayer of the Heart. He is the same Father Sergius whom Tolstoy wrote about, and is now over one-hundred-fifty years old. He hasn't eaten in forty years; he only drinks water. One of his close disciples is said to be the reincarnation of Jesus. It very well might be Brother Andrew! If Brother Andrew makes a phone call, he never gets a busy signal!

Chris has a tale he could tell, about the envelope cutter, but this is all peripheral, another form of adiaphora. The silly talk has nothing to do with the fact that Brother Andrew is tapped into a spiritual current of incredible magnitude which overflows into other people, and changes their lives forever.

The feelings generated by morning gathering carry Chris swiftly through the menial joyous tasks of his job. The energy he feels these days is astounding, as if all his life he'd been a

V-12 engine running on three or four cylinders and suddenly the rest have kicked in. Also, he can hardly believe how peaceful his life has become, and it is all Brother Andrew's doing. The small frustrations and humiliations of daily life seem to have dropped away, as if there were a protective shield around him. He doesn't misplace or lose things. He even finds things. When doing errands in Palo Alto his steps are led in such fashion as to eliminate encounters with speed freaks, or winos, or up-tight shop clerks, or the Crazy who involuntarily shouts "fuckshit" every thirty seconds. Nothing brings him down. He meets old friends on the street and they all remark how happy he looks lately.

Also, he feels embraced by his new friends. One night, Sarah phoned to say that Brother Andrew would be speaking that evening at Pacific High School. Would Chris care to join them? Of course, he said, and gave her directions to his house. They arrived in a little Volkswagen. John and Penny still seemed to have nothing to say. At Brother Andrew's request, Chris showed them through the house.

"Are these your cats?" Sarah asked.

"They used to be. My roommates have agreed to be their owners now."

"Why?"

"I'm not the most settled person."

"Me neither."

They all ended up on the deck. It was dark, but the redwoods towering up in front of them were still visible against the purple sky. A car went noisily past on Skyline.

"How much of this," Brother Andrew waved his arm at the trees, "belongs with the house?"

"Five acres."

"Really! Then why is the house so close to the road?"

"The rest of the property is too steep to build on."

"Ah, I see. Still, you must enjoy owning so much land."

"Hardly," Chris laughed. "This place is owned by a friend of mine. He's moved to Japan to study Zen. He rents it to us for about a quarter of what he could get for it."

"Ah! So, like me, you reap the benefits of someone else's spiritual search as well as your own!"

All this while, Sarah had stood with her hands on the railing, eyes closed, a slight smile on her lips. Brother Andrew touched her elbow to indicate they were going back inside. She opened her eyes. "I love the smell," she said. "I used to live about two miles from here." As she followed Brother Andrew into the house she put her hand on Chris' arm for a second.

They drove south on Skyline, and Brother Andrew asked if Chris was familiar with Pacific High School.

"Yes, a friend of mine used to teach pottery there." He refrained from saying the friend was Tamiko.

"Is it, as Penny says, all hippies and drug takers, and that sort?"

"More or less. I doubt if many of the kids will be there tonight, though. Most of them live down in the flatland. I don't know who your audience will be."

"I prefer not to call it an audience," Brother Andrew chuckled. "That strikes a bit too close to the truth. Tell me more about the school."

"It's what we call a free school. Rustic buildings, wild theories, kids who've been kicked out of public school or are too smart for it. That sort of thing."

"Ah, rather like Summerhill."

"Exactly. A psychedelic Summerhill. Day-glo paint and hobbits, sex and tofu and tree houses. Fewer redwoods than my place. Some meadows and boulders and a pond."

There were more students there than Chris had predicted, and many hill hippies, the type who avoid cities at all cost. Buckskin, beards, granny dresses, patchouli. They had stumbled, stoned, from their scattered cabins, domes, A-frames, yurts, and caves. They were chanting OM when Brother Andrew entered, and the vibes grew more intense until, after fifteen minutes, the room was awash.

89

"I first arrived in this country," Brother Andrew began, "in the summer of 1969. I landed in New York City and took a bus up to Ithaca to visit an old school chum. About halfway through that ride I began to feel I was back in India. The road was filled with groups of disheveled, dazed pilgrims with long hair, long dresses, carrying muddy sleeping bags, little bundles of possessions, some cooking utensils. Not India, maybe, but Europe in the Middle Ages. Not my image of sleek, rich America at all. My fellow passengers informed me that we were riding through the aftermath of Woodstock, but what that really meant was not clear to me at all until I arrived in Ithaca and read the newspapers. Later, of course, not far from here, you had Altamont, hell to Woodstock's heaven.

"This movement of yours, this great hippie revolution, is already crumbling, from your own excesses, Capitalist dilution, and government repression. So don't identify with it, or with chemical miracles, or you will go down with the space ship. Identify with eternity, become eternity, timeless bliss; everything else is mere appearance."

This raised some hackles, especially in one man in the back who looked, to Chris, like John the Baptist.

"Man," he asked, "have you ever even taken LSD?"

"No, and I've never been to North Dakota, either."

As the crowd was dispersing, the headmaster approached Brother Andrew and his group. His curly salt and pepper Afro bristling, shooting sparks, he thanked Brother Andrew. "If anybody wants to stick around, we're going to have a sweat."

"A what?" Brother Andrew asked.

"It's a Native American sauna. We have a sweat lodge up by our pond. You put hot rocks inside it, then take off your clothes and go inside. When you're scorching you scurry out and jump in the pond."

"Good Lord, in November?"

"Sure, would you like to try it?"

"Not I, thank you, but maybe . . .?" he asked, glancing over at Sarah and Penny. They looked at each other and giggled and said yes. John said yes and so did Chris.

Brother Andrew and the gaggle of brave souls walked through the darkness to the pond, to find a large bonfire tended by someone or something strikingly resembling a troll. The sweat lodge, nearby, looked like an igloo covered in dark carpet. The headmaster lit and passed some joints, but Brother Andrew's party declined.

The troll poked into the fire with a shovel, fishing out a large glowing rock covered in sparkling coals. He put the rock into a wire frame crate with a leather handle. Shoveling more glowing, sparkling rocks from the fire, he filled the crate. He picked it up about a foot off the ground and dropped it, creating pyrotechnic flying sparks, and a few oohs and aahs from those who were stoned. Then he hunkered the container through the narrow opening of the lodge. Everyone except Brother Andrew took off their clothes and crawled on hands and knees into the pitch dark space. The crate sat in a hole in the middle, the rocks still glowing slightly. The fine dirt of the floor stuck to hands and knees, and between toes. In the darkness the postulants arranged themselves in a circle around the rocks, sitting on the fine, sticky dirt. The troll lit a match, then a candle. He silently performed some ancient ritual with his hands and eyebrows and candle, then ladled water from an old metal pot onto the rock. There was a hissing sound while the air filled with mint-scented steam. It grew hot, and hotter . . . and hotter. Chris began to sweat; when he wiped the sweat from his face and arms the fine dirt stuck to them. He felt dirty, sticky, hot, wet, and wonderfully healthy. After a while someone could take it no longer and crawled across three or four bodies to the exit. Those still in the lodge heard a splash and a YEOWWW! Then they performed a general exodus and a wild rush to the wooden dock. When Chris plunged in he discovered that in fact on surfacing there was nothing, absolutely nothing he *could* do but yell YEOWWW! and quickly climb from the frigid water.

91

They stood in a circle around the fire, holding hands, letting the heat dry and warm them. Chris was almost opposite Sarah and watched as the flames cast moving shadows on her legs, her breasts, her long brown hair. Her eyes were closed; she was smiling, rocking back and forth slightly. He saw her as Youth; lovely, eminently desirable, but radiating bliss, not sensuality. He found himself praising Creation for the beauty of her body, and he felt beyond anything physical, in a realm where the phrase "the lineaments of gratified desire," which kept swimming through his mind, took on totally new meaning.

Sarah opened her eyes and smiled at him in a way to make him think she shared his thoughts. The circle broke up; people began to put on their clothes. John the Baptist walked over to Chris.

"You came here with that Limey asshole, didn't you?" he asked, nodding in Brother Andrew's direction.

"Yes," he answered, too dumbfounded to say anything else.

"Any idea how he knew I'm from North Dakota?"

"No," Chris said, "sometimes he just does stuff like that. I think maybe it's to let people know they belong with the Children of Light."

"No fucking way."

On the ride home they were silent. Sarah, Penny and Chris sat in the back seat. Sarah leaned her head against his shoulder and seemed to fall asleep immediately. Soon his shoulder began to ache, but he wouldn't have moved a muscle for all the gold in the Vatican. She woke up when they arrived at his house. He invited them in for tea, but Brother Andrew thought it too late. Sarah said she wanted to stand on the deck for just one minute, to smell the air, and Chris took her out there. She stood as before, hands on the railing, eyes closed. He asked her a question that had long been on his mind.

"Who put up that poster on Woodside Road for the lecture at Foothill?"

92

"I did."

"Why?"

"I don't know. I was driving out in Penny's car to visit my Mom, and that telephone pole just started glowing at me."

A moment later, when she left, she kissed him on the cheek and gave him a little hug. He stood there in the chill, hearing the car start up and drive away, and began to wonder in what direction, really, he was being led.

Four

Chris answered the ringing phone. "This is Andrew," he heard. Not Brother Andrew, just Andrew. "Penny, John and I are going up to the new Center in Berkeley this evening. Sarah, unfortunately, is a bit under the weather with chill or flu or something, probably caused by your native revels the other evening. I was wondering if you might come care for her, fetch tissues and that sort of thing. The baby will be here too."

"Of course," Chris answered.

"Good of you. Come about seven. Ta!"

The others were gone when he arrived. Sarah let him in. She was wearing a long flannel nightgown and woolen shawl. Her nose was red. She curled up on the sofa and covered her legs with an Afghan. The baby crawled among the round cushions on the floor, hiding and finding her milk bottle. Soon she fell asleep.

"I don't understand," Chris said, sitting on the floor, his back against the sofa, his head touching Sarah's leg. "Why are you all so nice to me? I feel like you're going out of your way to give me attention."

"You underestimate yourself." She put her hand on his shoulder. "Brother Andrew thinks you're the most promising disciple he has. Most of the others, he says, are here because it's a fad, or they want to feel a new high. But they really don't take it seriously, or they're too fiddled by drugs. I think he means strung out."

"God knows I've been fiddled. I wouldn't be sitting here if it weren't for LSD."

"Me neither. But Brother Andrew says some of us use drugs to learn and move ahead, and the rest just use drugs. Me, I'm flying pretty high right now on this cold medicine."

She was, in fact, wired in a dreamy sort of way, and they talked for over two hours, she sharing with him an effort to make some sense out of her past. She had grown up in Woodside, in a large Tudor house hidden from the road by a high hedge and a yard filled with live oak, eucalyptus and flowering acacia. Behind the house was a swimming pool bordered by eight tall palms which, full grown, had been brought in on a truck and planted using a back hoe and crane. Years later, when she had heard from Brother Andrew the story of Jesus' miracle, of the half blind beggar who saw men as trees walking, she remembered those palms, hanging on a stout chain, lumbering slowly through the air.

The estate had a barn, a large pasture, and four horses. From her bedroom, upstairs, Sarah could look down at the pool, the horses in the pasture, and across the few miles of valley to the Coast Range, to watch the fog push against its other side and tumble slantwise towards her through San Carlos Gap.

Her parents gave her books: Beatrix Potter, Winnie the Pooh, the Narnia Chronicles, George MacDonald, Black Beauty, The Secret Garden, the Oz books. By the time she was seven she could read them all to herself, over and over again. Her mental world was peopled with delight, as real to her as the paradise of her home with its frilly bedroom curtains, teddy bears, dolls, magic yellow trees, fiery gentle horses and distant fog-covered mountains.

Her mother sent her as a day student to the Woodside Priory, where she learned to spell correctly, to be lady like, to detest her plaid uniform and mandatory soccer. At home, she had her own television, record player, and telephone. When her older brother turned sixteen, he was given a Corvette.

The nuns tried to teach her to think and see clearly. At the age of about twelve, their work began to bear fruit. She clearly saw that her father, the vice-president of a bank in San Francisco, had nothing inside him except too much bourbon. She realized that her mother played too much bridge and was probably having an affair with the riding instructor. She realized that her brother, in spite of the Corvette, couldn't stand his parents. And she decided that her family's Catholicism meant nothing more than occasionally attending mass or displaying copies of *Ramparts* magazine on the living room coffee table.

When she was thirteen, the Beatles crossed the Atlantic, but by then she had mostly learned it all already. She and her girlfriends would ditch school, ride over to San Gregorio with high school guys to smoke dope, drink beer, groove on the ocean and the gulls, and find a nice private spot somewhere, out of the wind and under a blanket.

Then, one night in 1965 after a Rolling Stones concert in San Jose, she wound up at an Acid Test, and later sat outside in the back seat of a car, experiencing for God knows how long what is called the Clear Light. She never looked back. Within six months she was living in a commune near Skylonda with a lead guitarist who had once been a physics major at Cal Tech. Six foot four, he had red hair down to his waist, and had been continually stoned for seventeen and one half months.

The band was mediocre but had high hopes. It rehearsed in a garage about a mile from the commune. You could go there through the woods. Sometimes she would drop acid and walk over in the fog or rain and look at the ferns and mushrooms and up to the tops of the redwoods. Maybe she would find an old burned out stump of one of the giant trees that had been logged at the turn of the century. She would clean out the beer cans and candy wrappers, and sit inside it, feeling that she had lived for millions of years, millions of years ago.

She discovered that she could draw. Living in a commune fed your mind. People were into cosmic love, astrology, I Ching, yin and yang, Tolkien, the Book of the Dead and, of course, Rock and Roll, and the pictures it made in your mind. All of this went into her art. Her marijuana things were botanical, elfish, whimsical; on LSD she created swirling, bright galaxies which contained intricate oriental landscapes or wild, lurid orgies, hidden in what at first glance appeared simply a blob of paint. Stoner, her red haired lover, had promised her she could do the cover of the band's first album.

She also turned on to cooking, and vegetarianism. The kitchen was the social center of the house, a warm, trippy haven from the fog and rain and darkness outside. It had bundles of herbs hanging upside down on the walls, concert posters, and, on wooden shelves, large glass jars of rice, oats, millet, lentils, teas and wheat. They ground their own flour and baked righteous, heavy, natural bread. The spice racks went on forever.

While the women cooked, or baked, or washed the dishes, the men sat around the table on rickety wooden chairs and rapped cosmic raps. They received a constant stream of visitors, most of them groovy, who shared stories and joints, and bought or sold quantities of grass or LSD. The kitchen was a good place to be stoned, kneading dough or slicing vegetables or waiting, forever it sometimes seemed, for water to boil.

One afternoon Teddie the drummer and Danny were at the table and she was down on her knees, mostly inside one of the big cupboards, looking for more muffin tins, when she heard Spider's voice.

"Listen, man, that was the cops on the phone. Stoner's dead in a wreck on the Bay Bridge. It'll be fucking all over when they find those four kilos in his trunk. We've got to get the dope and the jailbait out of here fast."

She could feel it start, somewhere near her toes, and it seemed to take forever to reach her throat. By then, she was standing up, with Spider looking at her like she was a hallucination, and then the scream came out and just wouldn't stop for a long time.

Teddie took her down to a commune near Ben Lomond where some friends of his lived. A woman named Judy proved a big help. It was funkier than the house in Skylonda, though. The kitchen was never really very clean, and there was something wrong with the toilet so whenever you wanted to flush you had to fill a bucket from the bathtub and pour it into the toilet bowl. Sometimes people didn't bother. After about a week, Teddie started hanging around a lot and it became obvious he wanted to take Stoner's place. He had dirty curly hair and pig eyes and was a little bit fat and always kind of sweaty. With Judy's help, Sarah got him to back off.

One of the guys there went to UC Santa Cruz, and was really into Hermann Hesse. He dug her art work, and thought she might get behind drawing on speed. He gave her some, and after some more, she underwent the disconcerting experience of having her mind and body taken over by the astral self of Hieronymus Bosch. She had never even heard of Hieronymus Bosch, but after a while she got into it and she/Bosch began to cover the walls of her bedroom with an updated Garden of Earthly Delights. She stayed strung out, going without food or sleep for six days, and was half finished with the fourth wall when she collapsed. Judy took her to a hospital in San Jose, left her near the emergency room door, and split.

When Sarah was ready to leave the hospital, her parents brought her home, to her own room, with its view of the Coast Range where there were ferns, and fog, and fairy rings. For three months she did little but sleep, or read her childhood books, or play with a litter of kittens who lived in the barn. She was innocent again, secure in her surroundings, and glad of it. Her mother had the priest come around to talk to her, and she began going to mass some weekday mornings. Except that her mother kept trying to feed her meat, her parents were pretty good about the whole thing, insisting only that she have nothing to do with her old crowd. In the fall, in spite of the fact she had never finished high school, she started to audit two art courses at San Mateo Junior College. Her only friend and companion at this time was her cousin Penny, who had married John, a woodworker, and had a new baby. Sarah loved to hold the baby, or watch Penny nurse it.

Then one day John received a call from a friend of his in Topeka, an old college roommate, wondering if a Brother Andrew could come out and stay with them for a while, give some lectures, hold some meditations, that sort of thing. Brother Andrew was a high being, his friend assured him, and a constant joy to be around.

John and Penny said sure. Brother Andrew proved to be everything the friend had promised. Sarah helped the three of them set up some lectures around the Bay Area. Brother Andrew had been assigned the whole of America by Father Sergius, and had originally chosen Topeka because of its central location. When he discovered how the Bay Area received him, he decided just to stay. He gained many disciples in Berkeley, San Francisco, and Marin as well as the Peninsula, and could have chosen larger or more lavish headquarters, but opted to stay with Penny and John because "this is where God first sent me, and besides, they know how I like my tea prepared."

After a while, Sarah moved in too, and slept on a cot on the enclosed back porch, next to the water heater. She was a welcome presence, radiating perpetual bliss, allowing God to share her being the same way Hieronymus Bosch had, and it was God, not she, spreading the word, doing the work of the Children of Light.

About 10:30, Sarah said she needed to sleep. Chris tucked her in to her little cot next to the water heater, kissed her forehead, and turned out the light. Then he went back to the living room and entered into the Prayer of the Heart until Brother Andrew and the others returned.

Five

For the next six weeks, until just before Christmas, Chris happily gave a big chunk of his spare time to the Children of Light. He wrote letters, stuffed envelopes, made phone calls, helped arrange lectures. Then Brother Andrew went to Switzerland to see Father Sergius, and Sarah went with her mother for family Christmas in Baltimore. He would, he knew, miss them very much.

At the New Year, right after Brother Andrew returned, there was a gathering at Grace Cathedral in San Francisco. People from the outlying centers were there, as well as many newcomers. There must have been over two hundred people in the carpeted basement room. As always, Chris was enthralled just by basking in Brother Andrew's presence, and knew that all the others were also. When the evening ended, people began to stand up and search for their shoes and coats. A small group gathered around Brother Andrew. Sarah went over to Chris and hugged him, and he asked about her trip to Baltimore.

Then Brother Andrew spoke over the heads surrounding him. "Sarah, I forget the . . ." and he moved his finger around in a little circle.

"Oh, yes," she responded, then raised her voice. "Excuse me, I have an announcement." She was still holding Chris' hand, and looking at Brother Andrew, and the room grew quiet.

"Father Sergius thinks that it is time to spread the Light to Los Angeles. If anyone can help us do this, please let us know."

Brother Andrew, Father Sergius, God! They had been toying with him all along, hadn't they? The old carrot and stick, up and down, peek and boo. And now, he knew, to serve them, he was going to volunteer for something that no one in their right mind would want to do.

Mrs. Presto was upset when he gave her such short notice. She crushed out her cigarette, stomped around, harrumphed, told him so and should have known better and here less than two months, etc. She was slightly mollified when he told her his parents were in the middle of a divorce, and his mother needed his help. That his parents were getting divorced was in fact true. That his mother needed his help or even wanted him around was more questionable.

Brother Andrew gave him a small farewell tea party. When it finished, Brother Andrew hugged him and said "God bless you, brother. I'm sure you'll do the work well."

Sarah walked with him out to his car. "Did you hear? He called me brother!"

"I wish I could go with you," Sarah said. "But that's not the way it works, is it?"

The Southern California sprawl, Chris thought, lay on the earth like a scab on the back of a beautiful woman. Only in recent years, after moving away, had he realized how incredibly dreary it all was. While living there and growing up, its bland malignancy had been too much the tenor of his own mind and soul for him to notice. Bob's parents had said he could stay at their Surfside vacation beach house, so at least he would have the ocean to keep him sane.

Old Ford had made it all the way, bringing him and his few possessions, and had happily begun to add to the smog as Chris made his daily rounds. The work went well. The lectures planned themselves, had already been arranged by the Divine Hand. Chris merely confirmed the reservations. He would phone, go to see someone. Yes, an appropriate room is available for that evening. Luckily, we can advertise it in the monthly calendar, which goes to press tomorrow. And so on. A cinch. He even managed to arrange a lecture at the metaphysical bookstore in Santa Monica owned by the aunt of his old navy buddy Lars Sondberg.

After all the arrangements had been made, he had some flyers printed and put them around the colleges, and at book stores, health food stores, even on a few telephone poles. He also used them as press releases. He decided to go to San Diego for the day to visit old buddy Lars. He hoped he wouldn't miss any phone calls, but maybe San Diego would be fruitful ground also.

Lars wasn't much different from when they were together on the destroyer. Long hair now, of course, but his glasses still slid down his nose, a cigarette always dangled from the side of his mouth, and his pants still sagged around his seemingly nonexistent ass. He lived in a big run-down commune on a dingy street. He'd sold two paintings in three years. He dealt a little dope and peddled an underground newspaper on street corners. He fought constantly with his girlfriend. They called each other vile names, even in front of guests.

Everyone in the house acted a little paranoid. They knew that the cops, even the FBI, watched the house, because of the drugs, and because the paper's editor lived there. Revolutionaries, Communists. They had a large poster of Nixon that they threw darts at. One day, one of the street corner vendors who lived in the house had been wounded in the leg by a shot from a passing car.

Chris thought Lars was lost. Lars returned the compliment. "You've been sucked into a bunch of crap," he said. "You're as off the wall as my aunt. You've got your head wedged if you think God has a hand in running the affairs of this crummy planet."

What was wrong with Southern California? His old friend Randy, a newly-minted doctor with a newly-minted Corvette, was worried that Chris was getting too old to start a good career, gain any security, etc. His mother, naturally, whom he visited from time to time in Long Beach, was, as ever, also on his case. "Your Aunt Mae says he sounds like one of those preachers who always used to show up just in time for chicken dinner on Sundays. She's afraid maybe you've been brainwashed or something." The something, of course, was all those drugs Aunt Mae in Kansas had been hearing about on television. And how did he manage to make a living? Where did his money come from?

But he always felt much better when he returned to the beach house. He had removed the ashtrays, the bourgeois bric-a-brac, and the funny ha ha little signs, putting everything in a cupboard. He cleaned the place thoroughly, and turned it into a Temple. He had always been fond of the place, especially the screened porch that faced the sea. In high school, he and Bob had often sat there after a day of surfing. He saw the writing on the wall, however. The mile long string of happy old cottages was already starting to be replaced, here and there, by big fancy condos. They couldn't tear down the ocean, though.

Such joy! Such confusion! They arrived about nine o'clock in the evening. Brother Andrew, exhausted by the drive, went to bed before ten. Sarah and Penny were just the opposite: wired, giddy, unpacking the bags of groceries they had bought, snacking on this and that, exploring all the drawers and cupboards in the kitchen, chattering about the Beach Boys and blond surfers. It hurt Chris that Sarah was paying so little attention to him, but he told himself not to be silly.

"Where's Ashta?" he asked.

"At home," Penny said. "John's mother is visiting while we're gone." She giggled and did a little two step.

"You both seem stoned."

"Stoned?" Sarah looked at him cross-eyed. "Of course we're stoned. We've been stuck in a car with God all day." Both women cracked up at that one.

He turned to leave and then Sarah was beside him, holding his arm. "Please don't be upset, Chris. We've been working so hard for so long. We feel like we're on vacation."

103

She hugged him and everything felt all right again. Shortly, Sarah and Penny went off to bed. They were sharing the second bedroom. Chris, on the living room couch, tried to fall asleep but the sea was too loud. He thought about the details of the lectures, and imagined all the new souls joining the Children of Light. He too had worked hard and long, and he prayed that the week would be a success.

The next morning was beautiful, warm, a typical Southern California February day. Chris woke early, went walking on the beach, and returned to find an elaborate pancake breakfast being prepared. Brother Andrew sat in sunlight in the dining room, drinking tea, beaming.

"Look how pale Sarah and Penny and I are compared to you," he said, "and you've only been here a month. Take a memo someone. The Children of Light are moving their galactic headquarters to Southern California!"

"Ha!" Chris barked. "Wait until you've seen the place by daylight before you make up your mind. You'd be better off to choose Hawaii."

"I'll keep that in mind."

After breakfast they walked on the beach, or rather Chris and Brother Andrew walked, while Sarah and Penny skipped, hopped, and ran barefoot circles around them, singing Beach Boy songs and playing tag with the waves.

That evening, there were over two hundred people waiting for them at the Art Institute in Pasadena, students mostly. They chanted, and sat in silence, and something happened with the vibes that Chris had never experienced before. He stood in the back of the room. A little wave of spirit would flow to the front, where Brother Andrew was, bounce off the wall, then back towards him. He watched it moving through the crowd, like wind through a field of wheat.

Everyone, everyone, felt very high. Brother Andrew spoke about initiation, and asked Chris to give directions to Surfside. He did so, and got a few laughs. Then Brother Andrew asked "Out of curiosity, and so we can plan our day, how many of you intend to visit us tomorrow?" Over fifty people raised their hands. Over fifty people!

That night it again took Chris a long time to fall asleep. He lay there on the couch, mind ablaze. Now they were rolling! His work would bear fruit. Perhaps, in the sight of God, his life hadn't been such a sad waste after all!

Six

Chris awoke with a start the next morning to see the table lamp at the end of the couch hang in midair at a forty-five degree angle, then continue falling and smash into pieces when it hit the floor. The house rocked, creaking at its wooden joints. He had been through several of these in his life, but this must be the biggest.

Then Brother Andrew was standing next to him. "What's going on?"

"It's an earthquake," Chris said, as something fell in the kitchen.

"What should we do?"

"If it gets any worse, get Sarah and Penny and head outside."

"Here they are," Brother Andrew said as they came into the room.

The tremors continued, but with less intensity. It seemed almost finished; they felt a fairly big one, then a few small ones, then it was over. Aside from the lamp and some dishes, they were okay.

"Was that a bad one?" Brother Andrew asked.

"That depends on where its center was. How far away."

Penny went into Brother Andrew's room and brought out the little radio, and for the rest of the morning they listened as the news reports came in. A big one, centered in the San Gabriel Valley. Very few deaths, but some buildings had fallen, some freeway overpasses collapsed, and many roads were cracked and closed. A dam in San Fernando had also cracked, and people downstream were being evacuated.

106

Sarah and Penny were in a mild state of shock, sitting around, not talking much. Chris cooked oatmeal, also served toast, marmalade and tea.

"Do you think all those people will come today?" Penny asked.

"It will be difficult for them," Brother Andrew replied, and he was right. They took turns staying at the house while the others walked on the beach, but only one person arrived. Her name was Julie Blodgett. About twenty, mousy, she worked in a bank in Glendale and had been at the gathering in Pasadena the night before. Spunky, she had skipped work and braved the traffic hazards to drive down and be initiated.

That evening they went to the gathering at U.C. Irvine. Four people attended. One of them wanted to know why God causes earthquakes and Brother Andrew answered "To shake us up. To make us think."

Four people. Nobody. All Chris' work in pieces, like the shattered lamp. He didn't know if he should laugh or cry. Lars' aunt called and cancelled the Friday night talk at her bookstore. Wednesday night at UCLA and Thursday at Long Beach State were more crowded, but still only six new people came for initiation. Sarah and Penny were depressed. Brother Andrew took it in stride.

Friday afternoon, all their business finished, they drove out to a still undeveloped part of Orange County, to the Monastery of the Vedanta Society. There was a special three day something or other going on and the monks wouldn't even let them in. They were allowed, however, to stroll around the grounds, and found a pleasant little nook filled with sun, the sound of a million joyous birds, and the odor of honeysuckle. Brother Andrew talked about Ramakrishna, Vivekananda, Yogananda and all the others. Chris knew he had some connection to India, but had never heard much about it.

"It took seventy five years for their efforts to really bear fruit in this country. Rome wasn't built in a day. We have no right to be discouraged. You have done good, hard work, Chris. I thank you from my heart."

107

They went into silence. The birds, the sun, the honeysuckle, all were glorious. Chris was with the two people he felt closest to in the entire world. Then it happened. Brother Andrew might have touched his elbow, he later thought, but he couldn't be sure. Maybe it came direct from Ramakrishna, or God. But a jolt, a shock of electric honey went through his entire body. Intense, total, unlike anything he had ever experienced. Proof, proof absolute of the unbearable holiness that fills every atom of the universe. He would never doubt again!

He could still feel the afterglow of that reward Friday night, when they had a gathering for the new initiates. Only three of them showed up. Brother Andrew called them the nucleus of a great future, and urged them to assist Chris in forming a new center.

Saturday morning, after many hugs, Brother Andrew, Sarah and Penny got into the little Volkswagen and drove away. Chris waved to them, one last time, then walked on the beach, watched some surfers in wet suits for a while, and returned to the cottage. He did the dishes, tidied up, and went to sit on the screened porch. He could only stay here a few more weeks, he knew, before Bob's parents would start using the cottage for themselves on weekends. Where could he go? That was minor, though. What was major was that he had lost it. Totally. Just the day before he had had the most amazing experience of his life. Today he didn't know how he could carry on. He could only hope for the best.

And hope for the best. Everything, he thought two weeks later after he had moved into Julie Blodgett's living room, does work for the best. If only we could understand it. But why does God make it all so hard to decipher?

He and Julie seemed to be all that remained of the Children of Light in Los Angeles. In those two weeks he had held three gatherings in Surfside, and the other six initiates had made lame excuses not to come. He found himself pouring out for Julie his frustrations and his need to find someplace to live besides back home with his mother, and she offered to let him stay in her apartment for a while.

Julie, Chris thought, was an interesting contradiction. Very much like a flower waiting to bloom, both physically and spiritually. She had long blonde hair and a pretty but frightened face, with the eyes of a loner. Her body, her movements, seemed still slightly adolescent, not fully woman. She lived in a plastic and plywood apartment in Glendale about six blocks from her job at the bank. Her apartment, job, clothes, all very straight. But she had a great rock and roll collection, which Chris listened to a lot while Julie was at work.

She had grown up in Detroit, and went to Wayne State for a year before moving West. He asked her "but why Glendale?" and she answered "It's cheaper than Pasadena, and compared to Detroit it's Heaven. Just try to imagine what it's like to be cooped up in a dark little house in a crummy neighborhood on New Year's Day, with noisy cousins and drunk aunts and uncles, and a ten below blizzard outside; to see the Rose Parade on TV, and people in shirt sleeves in the sun at the Rose Bowl. It's like a vision of paradise."

He introduced her to vegetarianism and baking their own bread. They had a gathering every morning before she went to work, and one every evening. Chris was content, he guessed, as an exile in Southern California, living in forced inactivity. He wanted to set up another series of lectures, but Brother Andrew couldn't be pinned down on any definite dates. So Chris took long walks, listened to rock and roll, and read dusty old religious books from the local library. He enjoyed his brother/sister relationship with Julie. Sometimes on weekends they would go to Surfside or Huntington Beach, walk, and watch the surfers. He kept discovering new qualities in her. She came from a strong union family, and was more aware of what made society tick than one would think. She could joke about her flat chest, about her fear of driving on freeways, about her ridiculous job at the bank.

109

Though she could also joke about the Children of Light, her spiritual growth moved full speed ahead.

But then it happened. He had just stretched out on the couch one night when Julie came from her room and sat on the floor in the darkness next to him. She put her hand on his arm. "Will you come to bed with me?"

It took him a long time to answer. He couldn't think how to say it. Finally he said "I'm sorry, Julie. I thought you understood that I'm trying to be celibate, like Brother Andrew. I'm trying to devote myself completely to God. I hope I haven't done anything to mislead you."

"No, I just thought . . . it seemed like, you know, that if people see the God in each other, that they . . . All, uh, all the time I was growing up, it never seemed to me the nuns were happy. Some of them were just plain sick, and took it out on us."

"Do you want me to move out?"

"No, of course not...."

After several minutes she stood up, and kissed him on the forehead. Then she went back into her room and closed the door. He felt awful, as if he were in some way mistreating her. It didn't seem like any great spiritual victory. And what, he wondered, if the question had come from Sarah rather than Julie?

He went to the living room window, and saw that it had begun to rain. He watched it fall in the arc of the street lamp and in the headlights of the cars that drove past. Their tires made that wet, squeeshy sound on the pavement. He went to get a drink of water, then returned to the window. Most likely it wouldn't even be worth it. He hadn't made love in a long while, and Julie's responses would probably be awkward, girlish.

He went to the door of her room and opened it. She was still awake, reading by the light of a small tensor lamp. Her pajamas were covered with little baseballs and mitts and bats and baseball caps. She set her book down on the bedside table.

110

And then the phone rang. Since he'd moved in, almost all of the calls had been about the Children of Light. He'd better answer it.

"Andrew here. I'm sorry to call so late. How are you?"

"Brother Andrew! . . . . I'm, uh, fine."

"Good. Incredible things are happening here. We've rented a large center near downtown Palo Alto, on Bryant Street. It's a Queen Anne, with a marvelous turret. I'm in the turret, of course, but there's a small room with a balcony overlooking the back yard. I'm saving it for you. The back yard needs quite a bit of work, by the way. I hope you have a green thumb. Also, we're forming a new organization. I need your brains, your skill. Can you come tomorrow or the next day?"

"Give me a minute, at least, to think. Why start a new organization? What about the Children of Light?"

"I've looked into that. If we try to incorporate as the Children of Light we will all have to register as foreign agents or something. The new group will be called Y.E.S. – Youth for an Enlightened Society! We're going to change the entire country. Say you'll come."

"Of course I'll come. Not tomorrow, the next day. What about Los Angeles, though?"

"Los Angeles will still be there when we're ready for it. Sarah sends her love. Remember, 245 Bryant. Do you need directions?"

"Hardly. It's my old stomping grounds."

"Good. God bless you. Ta!"

Julie took it well. Chris couldn't have known, she said. But it was awfully sudden. Maybe she would move up to Palo Alto someday.

When he called to say goodbye to his mother before heading north, she didn't take it at all well. To please her he had signed up for a Civil Service Test. Serf apprentice or some such category, and now he was skipping out on it. "You'll never get another chance," she said. "You burn all your

111

bridges. It's like you don't *want* to amount to anything. Do you ever stop and think what's going to happen to me?"

He kept trying to say goodbye. "Go ahead," she whined. "Run after that phony baloney Jesus of yours. At least I'll be able to face my friends again. Dorothy Morris said the last time she saw you, you looked just like her nephew, with your scruffy hair and the hole in your sweater, and he's in jail for selling heroin. Believe me, Dorothy said, don't let them tell you they can get along without a job and still be on the up and up. Oh, it's all right, I said, he's just scrounging off that little whore."

He finally broke away, but failed to arrive in Palo Alto when promised. In King City, Old Ford gave up the ghost. Her ticker just plumb wore out. He sold her to a junk yard for fifteen dollars, exactly the price of his motel room. The next day he hitch hiked on up to Palo Alto, carrying all his worldly possessions with him.

Seven

Idleness ceased to exist. There was only energy, God's energy, and manifestations of divine love. The house needed much work. It was a mess. The previous tenants, a cell of the Revolutionary Union, had been busted and evicted. The dope charges were a clear frame up, but once the cops were inside they found the illegal weapons, and that charge would probably stick. The Children of Light repainted every room, including all six bedrooms, fixed the broken windows, cleaned and waxed the beautiful hardwood floors, and thoroughly banished the meat grease from the oven and around the burners. Brother Andrew wandered around helpfully, full of encouraging remarks.

Spring had arrived. Blue skies and flying white clouds. Chris cleaned up the back yard and broke his back digging ground for a garden. Sarah's mother brought over two barrels of horse manure. Chris showed Sarah how to prepare the soil and plant seeds. They put in lettuce, chard, spinach, carrots, radishes, and eight mounds of zucchini. They bought some strawberry plants.

The days were warm. One afternoon, working with his shirt off, he stood near Sarah as she planted lettuce seeds. She was wearing one of those tank top shirts, and looking down he could see a fine covering of sweat and dust on her breasts, reminding him of that night at the sweat lodge. He was very happy. After planting, worn out, the two of them sat in silence, holding hands, listening to the joyous praise of the birds.

All six bedrooms were full. Brother Andrew, Sarah, and Chris. Then Roger, who had more or less been put in charge of cooking and buying food. Justin, who worked in a bank on

University Avenue, coordinated the Bay Area gatherings and sold the little pamphlet that Brother Andrew had just published. And then Gerrie, who worked at Lockheed on computers or something. She liked to talk about people's auras. Chris thought she was paying most of the rent. She owned, of all things, a new yellow Porsche.

Chris had been appointed gardener, and also worked on setting up Youth for an Enlightened Society, Inc. The paper work proved extremely tedious, but he knew it would be worth it. They would still be Children of Light, too, as so many people were already attached to the name. He had only been gone two months, but the organization seemed to have doubled in size. He told Brother Andrew he would need to find a part time job. Andrew laughed and said nonsense, those who do God's work are taken care of by God. Yours is not to worry about money, or rent, or other adiaphora.

Chris wondered about Penny and John, why they didn't come to gatherings. Brother Andrew, it turned out, had told them to take a break, to just be together as a family for a while, to recharge their batteries.

"How is Julie?" Brother Andrew asked one day as they were looking at the garden. Everything had sprouted, and was about one inch high.

"She's fine. Really growing spiritually. She's talking about moving up here, to be closer to you."

"To be closer to you, you mean." Brother Andrew laughed, and Chris blushed. "She'll need to stay down there, though, for a while, at least until the Y.E.S. training retreat."

Chris let that one pass. Brother Andrew had more irons in the fire than anyone could keep up with. "Uh . . . , it did start to become a little complicated. I . . . uh . . . we . . ."

"Oh, cut the crap. You're such a Puritan. What do you want me to do, slap your wrist?"

A strange thing was happening. Brother Andrew and Chris were becoming friends, almost, dare he say it, equals. Chris no longer saw him as someone on a distant pedestal. They worked well together forming Y.E.S. They matched wits and puns. The bad part of this was losing that sense of awe, that overwhelming feeling in the top of his head whenever they were together. The good part was that the divine seemed to be slowly revealing itself in everyone or everything he saw, heard, or touched. Brother Andrew had led him up a mountain, and now was letting him see what existed on that higher level. They trusted each other implicitly.

For Chris' twenty-eighth birthday, they had a little party. Sarah baked a cake. Gerrie had a theory about seven year cycles. Chris was just beginning a new, hypo-zodiacal, trino-spherico-galacto spiritual journey. He saw it as much simpler than that. He had merely given himself to God.

Here they are, four hundred Children of Light at a weekend retreat in the Santa Cruz Mountains. At a scout camp. Has this place, Chris wonders, ever seen a zonked out group of God Scouts like this, spending a whole weekend saying the Prayer of the Heart, chanting, eating simple food? At the closing session, Brother Andrew is beginning to speak. "We are going to start a revolution," he says, and the little guy with the ferret eyes who has been sitting in the corner all weekend begins to take notes. "Mark this well, however," he looks over at the little guy, "I'm speaking not of a revolution with guns, or good guys and bad guys, but a revolution of the Spirit. America is the most religious country in the world, but her Spirit is asleep, or sleepwalking through jungles in Asia, through ghettoes, through smog.

"We will start with the Prayer of the Heart. From thence comes fearlessness, absolute trust in God. That's all we need. Organizing skills, non-violence, how to correct injustice – all those things flow naturally from trust, absolute trust in God. There are four hundred of you in this room. One month from now, one hundred of you will return here for a two week session of meditation and preparation, and then you will set out alone for one hundred cities throughout the country to form Y.E.S. chapters and, poor and homeless yourselves,

115

begin work among the poor, the homeless, but also among the rich, the powerful. You will walk in the footsteps of the saints.

"Ask yourself, in the next weeks, if you are among the one hundred who will answer this call, who have been foreordained all along to be part of this great work. Ask the question of the deepest, purest part of yourself. And if the answer is yes, then go, put your affairs in order, and lay down your wearisome habits and attachments. You might encounter more suffering than you think you can bear, but the work begins here, I tell you. The great change in the direction of this planet begins here, and now. Who has ears, let him, or her, hear."

What a bubbling stew, all these preparations for the long retreat! People came and went constantly. Chris and Sarah were hoping to have the garden wholly thinned, cultivated and mulched so that Justin, while the rest were at the Y.E.S. training, would only have to water it. Chris struggled to finish the I.R.S. paperwork for their nonprofit exemption. He was the official Secretary-Treasurer of Y.E.S. They had seven hundred dollars in the bank and a shiny chrome handled tool that embossed their corporate seal on official documents. Brother Andrew was President, and Sarah Vice-president.

They were so busy that Brother Andrew had stopped going to the other centers, which now sent carloads of people to him once or twice a week. Palo Alto had gatherings every night in the large living room. The crowds often spilled over into the dining room. And so many surprises! Gerrie quit her job to become part of the first Y.E.S. wave. Roger also was going, and Chris and Sarah of course. Brother Andrew spoke of sending Chris to Honolulu, but hadn't decided yet if he could part with him. Chris was torn, wanting to go there but not wanting to leave Brother Andrew or Sarah. He'd been exiled once already.

Brother Andrew often huddled in conference. So many came to him, unsure if they were called to serve or not, afraid to give up jobs and security, looking for him to answer their

116

fears. He turned most of them back on themselves, the decision to be made on the altar of their hearts. Chris understood their struggle, was full of compassion, felt lucky he had nothing left to give up.

The ludicrous, too, stalked them. The little guy with the ferret eyes came around so much that Brother Andrew put Chris in charge of him. He pretended to be a disciple, and asked naïve questions like "has Brother Andrew ever carried the Light to Russia?" Ferret Eyes really thought he was fooling them. If he was the best that the F.B.I. or C.I.A. could come up with, America was in big trouble.

Eight

Here they were, one hundred and ten of them, on the threshold of a new age, a new earth. They were all to receive a new, second level Prayer of the Heart. They were all to learn to lead simple yoga and meditation classes. Chris started growing a beard. Julie was there. She had quit her job, given up her apartment, car, everything. Chris hoped she had done it for the right reasons.

There were some rules for the two weeks. No alcohol, no drugs, no sex. It surprised Chris to hear some groans from the crowd at this last one. Brother Andrew explained why it was necessary, and that it was only for two weeks. He would not presume to create different areas for male and female. People could sleep where they wanted, but shouldn't share sleeping bags. The large room pretty much divided between the sexes, though. Everyone realized it would be easier that way.

Someone had given Brother Andrew a fancy super 8 camera, and he wanted Chris to film as much of the Y.E.S. training as possible. Chris tried to get out of it, but Brother Andrew insisted, on the grounds that he had already bought twenty-five rolls of film. Part of Chris enjoyed using his old technical skills, creating well-framed scenes of meditation and lively action shots, but another part of him wished the camera wasn't stuck between him and the here and now.

At times, the scene seemed a little like the Navy. People lining up for showers, for chow, living in close quarters, clothes hanging from pegs. Indoctrination. They were preparing to sail uncharted seas, but they had the best navigator of all. And what a voyage it was! The best part was just sitting, all of them in silence, Brother Andrew on the raised hearth in front of the fireplace, where everyone could see him. Sometimes Brother Andrew would begin a song, a chant, and after a while everyone would join in, in unison, like a well-drilled maneuver.

Once, during free time, he and Julie walked in the forest. She was excited about doing God's work, and wondering what city she would be sent to. He couldn't imagine, she said, how free she felt after quitting her job. Oh yes he could, he told her. She surprised him by apologizing for the night she had come on to him, and he didn't quite know how to respond.

That night, though, after the gathering, the singing, the guitar serenade, he was drifting off in the darkness when someone plopped a sleeping bag down next to him, wriggled into it, and settled a hand on his shoulder. He was sure it was Julie, but then Sarah's voice quietly said "good night," and those two words nourished his soul like a soft rain. "I love you," he said into the darkness.

Two mornings later, Brother Andrew called Chris into his room. Julie was in jail in San Jose. No one had even noticed she was gone. She had left the night before and hitched down out of the mountains. The highway patrol picked her up a little after midnight, ran her through the files, and found a warrant for an unpaid parking citation. So they locked her up. Eighty dollars would spring her.

Brother Andrew gave Chris a hundred dollar bill and the keys to Gerrie's Porsche. "Once she's free of that dreadful place, find out what the matter is. Be gentle with her, and see if she won't come back to us."

Chris had never driven such a car before. He was an expert at winding down mountain roads, as was the Porsche, but still, he felt ridiculous. He didn't belong in a car like this.

He'd expected a big waiting room littered with Styrofoam cups. High ceilings, slow moving fans, spittoons, old drunks sleeping it off on scarred wooden benches, children crying, mothers weeping, cops processing people in handcuffs, the stale smell of cigarettes. No way. Jail was modern, up to date. Built like a brick shithouse, no windows, ready for the

119

Revolution. He walked into the little foyer and spoke through thick plate glass to a bored, bouffant hairdo. She sent him down the hall to door three. He entered, found himself in a tiny room, and heard the door click behind him in a way that let him know he was locked in. He tried it anyway, just to make sure.

Another plate glass window, with a cop behind it. "I'm here to pay the fine for Julie Blodgett."

"May I see your driver's license?"

"Why?"

"We can't release her to you without identification."

He knows he should protest. But he just wants them both out of the place. He puts his license through a little trap door and the cop goes off somewhere, obviously to run him through the files. He's not worried, he hasn't done anything wrong. But what if . . . what if he had a parking ticket once that blew off the windshield? What about mistaken identity, maybe some Feldkirchen wanted in New Jersey for armed robbery? The cop doesn't come back and doesn't come back, and he tries the locked door once again.

The officer returned, gave him back his license and also a form to fill out, and took his money. Then he was let out of his cage, sent through another door, and down a long hall. He waited for twenty minutes until Julie appeared. She was sullen, withdrawn, didn't want to talk. He drove to a coffee shop and they ordered lunch. She took out her checkbook.

"I wouldn't have called up there if they'd have taken my check, but they only take cash. I didn't have anybody else to call." She insisted on writing a check, so he told her to make it out to Y.E.S.

"What's the matter Julie? What's wrong?"

"You really don't know, do you?"

"Is it because of Sarah? I'm sorry Julie, but . ."

"I've just had my eyes opened, that's all. There's no point in talking to you about it."

"Will you come back to the training? I'm sure we can work it out."

"No, I'll find somewhere to go."

"Look. I'll take you back to the Center in Palo Alto. You can stay there and maybe, in a few days, you'll decide to come back. Justin would bring you up there, I'm sure."

She agreed to stay in Palo Alto, but still he couldn't get her to talk about how she felt or why she left. He was sure it was because of Sarah and he was sorry. But what a relief to go back up to the mountains, to the training! The scout camp had become his whole universe. He'd forgotten about freeways, jails; the reminder had been an unwanted interruption. He gave Brother Andrew a short report, and handed him Julie's check, the change from the coffee shop, and the keys to the Porsche. Brother Andrew told him to keep the change.

The next afternoon Chris helped Brother Andrew match people with the city they were to be sent to. Brother Andrew was profoundly ignorant of American Geography, yet they would look at the map, Chris would describe the city, its state and region, and Brother Andrew would choose someone to go there. The choice always seemed unerring, fitted the character and Karma of each person like a glove. A minor skill, probably, picked up somewhere on the astral plane.

Imagine. One hundred and nine people, about to cover the entire U.S., to bring good works, healing, and the Light. Like St. Francis, or Johnny Appleseed. Traveling without money, some by car, but most on foot and by thumb, trusting completely in God, and in the training Brother Andrew had given them, in the knowledge that they were founding a great spiritual movement that would change the course of the country.

Chris would not go to Honolulu. He was being assigned to San Jose, but his main job would be to stay in Palo Alto and coordinate the support for the Y.E.S. workers on the road. And he had a car! A little VW Bug. Jim Nelson, from Berkeley, was leaving it for him. Jim had been assigned to Salt Lake City and decided he would rather live without it. Jim's grandfather

121

had once been the head gardener of the Mormon Temple there. God works in strange ways.

It had begun! And with a surprise. They weren't supposed to leave until Sunday, but Saturday morning after breakfast Brother Andrew gathered them all together. "Like children, waiting for Christmas, the anticipation is almost unbearable, isn't it? And then, the presents opened too quickly, the disappointment because that's all there is; the mind, wandering. Let's avoid all that, shall we? Everyone up, pack your things, go. Now. No long farewells. We are all part of each other anyway. No dilly-dallying, no sadness. And no side trips. Everyone, from here, go to your city. Now. Don't go back to Berkeley, or San Francisco, or to your parents' house for a few days. The work starts now. Here. Drop us a postcard when you arrive. God bless you all."

A few hours later, the building was empty. Only Jim Nelson and Chris, doing the last cleaning up, picking up whatever was left behind, clearing out the refrigerators.

In a way, Chris wished the training could have gone on forever.

Jim and Chris had just been packing the leftover food into the little VW when a car drove up to the building. Out crawled Mike and Phil, two guys Chris knew slightly from the Berkeley Center, and a man in a white robe like Brother Andrew's. "Where is everyone?" Mike asked.

"They've all headed out," Chris answered.

"I thought they weren't leaving until tomorrow!"

"Brother Andrew changed the plan."

Mike looked upset. Phil started inside.

"I am Brother Pierre," the white robed man said, with a French accent. "This is all very unfortunate." He had a long chin and for some reason made Chris think of old woodcuts of John Calvin. Brother Pierre too started to go inside.

"Look," Mike said, "Brother Andrew has been up to some weird stuff, and it's all starting to come out. John told

122

Switzerland about Penny, and Brother Pierre was sent here to replace him and try to fix up the mess. I hope it's not too late."

"What's wrong?"

"Everything. He gets people to give him all their money. We know a few people who've resisted. But a lot of those who went to this Y.E.S. thing gave him everything. What about you guys?"

"I gave him six hundred dollars," Jim said, "and am going to leave the VW behind. But that's part of the trip, giving up everything and trusting in God!"

"Yeah, but Brother Andrew gets rich, not God. What about you, did you give him anything?"

"I didn't have anything to give him. What makes you think he wasn't going to use the money for Y.E.S. work?"

"Because he knew he was in trouble, and that it was all over. And because he cleaned out all his papers and stuff, everything out of his room when he came here."

"What do you mean, he knew it was all over?"

"Father Sergius found out he has a kid in Topeka. And he's been screwing all sorts of women around here. Judy Evans in San Francisco, and Laurie in Berkeley, and Penny, and Sarah . ."

Chris grabbed Mike by the arm. "Who says?"

"Judy, and Laurie, and Penny."

"What about Sarah? Who says?"

"Penny. Sometimes the three of them would do it together."

He let go of Mike. "Fuck this. I don't believe any of it."

"None of us believed it. All we could see were the white robes and the holy vibes. But we've been had. And he did it so smooth, and could keep all this money stuff under cover because he only had two accomplices, Sarah and that guy Chris."

"What guy Chris?"

"That Chris Feldkirchen guy."

"I'm Chris Feldkirchen!"

"You are . . .? Uh, sorry man . . .Uh, I've only met you once, I think. I didn't recognize you . . . Is your beard new? Shit. This is all a surprise to you?"

"Totally."

"All of it?"

"Yes, all of it."

"Shit, man, let's go talk to Brother Pierre."

"We thought you were part of it, you know, because your room was emptied out too." Brother Pierre gave off serious, solid vibes, like a rock, but Chris couldn't sense anything rarefied or high about him.

"I don't own anything," Chris said. "Everything of mine is in that VW."

"I see. And do you know the whereabouts of any money?"

"There's about seven hundred dollars in a checking account. Brother Andrew and I can both write checks on it, so I don't know if it's still there or not. What about Sarah's room? Was it cleared out?"

"No," Mike said, "her stuff is still there."

"Then you're just taking Penny's word for it."

"What time did Brother Andrew leave this morning?" Brother Pierre asked.

"About ten-thirty, when all the others did."

"Who was with him?"

"Sarah. They were in Gerrie's Porsche."

"And you," Brother Pierre asked softly, "which of the female disciples did you have sex with?"

Chris didn't answer, just turned and headed out the door toward the VW to get his things.

"Many people think you were also having sex with this Sarah."

Mike chimed in, "That's probably what she and Brother Andrew wanted them to think."

Chris had his sleeping bag and little suitcase and a sack with the twenty five rolls of film, and was starting to walk down the dirt road to the highway. He left the camera in the car. It wasn't his anyway.

"Remember," Brother Pierre called after him, "you are still a Child of Light, and Father Sergius loves you. There is room for you at the Center if you wish. We will need to find out about that bank account. Can you give us a phone number or something to know how to reach you?"

"I'm sure you're clairvoyant enough to find me if you want."

Some of those disciples, those frail human disciples, couldn't even follow Brother Andrew's last order. A dozen of them stopped at the Berkeley Center for a farewell party, and were told not to proceed further. Gerrie stopped back at Palo Alto to pick up something she needed. When she found out what was happening, she flipped out completely and put herself in the hospital. She had given Brother Andrew seventeen thousand dollars and signed over title to the Porsche. Thirty of the Y.E.S. crew were able to be rounded up, and the rest would be recalled as soon as they made contact.

Julie figured Chris would be at the house on Skyline that he had told her so much about, and phoned there a week or so after the debacle. Sarah's mother had come by to remove all of Sarah's things, she told him. Brother Pierre needed him to go to the bank. Julie, Justin and Brother Pierre came up to the house to get him. The seven hundred was still in the account. Chris closed it down and the money was transferred to the Children of Light. It was clear to Chris that Justin and Julie were pretty much a new couple.

They wanted him to come back to the Center for the day, and he agreed, because he needed to see for himself. He looked at the empty bedrooms. He worked in the garden until supper, weeding, cultivating, and watering. The lettuce and greens were ready to eat. The radishes were all woody and pulpy. There would soon be enough zucchini for all the starving children in China.

They ate supper. It seemed formal, serious, not full of fun like when Brother Andrew was there. Then there was a gathering, of about thirty people. A large picture of Father Sergius now adorned the wall; people faced it and with completely straight expressions sang:

> *L'amour, c'est le Père Serge.*
> *Lumiere, c'est le Père Serge.*
> *Le Père Serge, Le Père Serge.*

Chris looked at the picture and remembered that Sarah once said Father Sergius reminded her of Heidi's grandfather, the old Alm-uncle. Chris felt nothing. There was no joy, no high humming spirituality anywhere in the room. The people, even Julie, all looked like robots. The Prayer of the Heart was now done with eyes open, gazing at the picture. Chris purposely closed his eyes, but the Prayer wouldn't come. At the end, Brother Pierre delivered a few bourgeois moral precepts. People nodded sagely.

Justin would drive him home. Julie asked if she could come along, but Brother Pierre wouldn't allow it. Chris walked down the sidewalk to the car, certain he would never enter that house again.

On the way up from the flatlands, Justin asked if he had any idea where Brother Andrew was. None at all, Chris said. They had talked to a lawyer, Justin said. Apparently, Brother Andrew had done nothing fraudulent. In all cases so far people had surrendered their money and possessions voluntarily, for the good of their souls. Lawyers had tried to sue the Catholic Church for fraud before, make it prove there was a heaven, and had always lost the cases. Perhaps Brother Andrew could be reasoned with, however, persuaded to return some of the loot.

Home, he climbed out of Justin's car. "If you do hear where he is, you'll let us know, won't you?"

"Certainly."

126

The day after his visit to the Center, he could stand it no longer. He picked up the phone and dialed. Sarah's mother answered.

"This is Chris Feldkirchen. Is Sarah there?"

"No, Chris, she isn't. I have a message for you though."

"You do? What is it?"

"I'm supposed to give it to you in person, to be sure it's really you. We met once, you'll recall, when I brought over the manure."

"I'm up on Skyline, and don't have a car. Are you sure you can't just tell me?"

"Well, Sarah was very insistent."

"I assure you I'm me. The time we met, remember? Your name is Letitia. Your eyes are the same color as Sarah's; you were wearing your hair in a bun. You have a yellow Buick. You talked about your son, who dropped out of Notre Dame and was going to some hippie college in Ohio. You were worried Sarah wasn't getting enough vitamins. . . . okay?"

"Yes," she laughed. "It's you. But what I'm to tell you is absolutely confidential, not to be shared with others."

"Of course."

"Good. Can you please send the Y.E.S. film to Sarah in care of General Delivery, Honolulu?"

"That's the message?"

"Yes."

"That's all?"

"Yes, it is. I know so little about what is going on. Penny won't talk to me about it. All Sarah would say is that Brother Andrew is very tired and needs a vacation."

"I'm afraid I don't know any more than you do, except that this new Brother Pierre is a jerk."

"That's what Sarah said Brother Andrew says. It all sounds very much like when my husband's bank was bought up by a competitor. It can get so nasty."

"Well, thank you . . ."

"Chris?"

"Yes?"

"If you hear from her will you let me know?"

"Certainly."

He'd shot all 25 rolls, but hadn't had them developed yet. He hitched down to a lab that could do it in twenty-four hours, then went the next day to pick them up. He still had his old super 8 viewer with a four inch screen. Twenty-five rolls. Seventy-five minutes of action. He edited for two days. An editor, he remembered, is like a god. A sloppy god will make the shots too long, will keep those three or four frames before the hand actually begins to move to the doorknob, will fail to imagine the myriad more telling ways in which the scenes can be arranged. A real god, well, let's say if God were real, God would never make a bad cut, always maintain some twisted kind of continuity, have no compunctions about leaving yards and yards on the cutting room floor, or playing around to create a finer reality than ever existed. A Real God could maybe even throw in a happy ending.

The film turned out well. Twenty minutes long, full of vibrant, happy, very high people doing odd things: standing on their heads, climbing trees, washing dishes, holding hands in one large circle, hugging each other, saying the Prayer of the Heart. And everywhere, beaming, approving, the white robed spectre of Brother Andrew. If he cranked the film through the viewer faster than normal, the motion would speed up, jerky, like old black and white movies of happy people taken on the eve of World War I.

Sarah was there too, in many shots. One marvelous close-up of her face. Exactly three seconds. Fifty-four frames. He looked at them, one at a time, trying to decide which was most like her. Each was slightly different, as a Mona Lisa smile changed to an embarrassed grin, and at the end into something almost resembling guilt. It was then he decided he would deliver the film in person. He borrowed four hundred dollars from Bob, and bought a one way ticket to Honolulu.

128

Nine

When he first arrived in Honolulu, he stayed with his childhood friend Irene and her husband. He knew he had worn out his welcome the last time he was there, the time he had met Tamiko, so he promised he would find a room as soon as possible. The first day, though, he used their phone, making calls to churches, bookstores, health food stores, anywhere he could think of where someone might have seen a man in a white robe. The next day he found a cheap room in a boarding house in the Jungle, a run-down area of central Waikiki rapidly being replaced by high-rise hotels and condos. And the day after that, he sat on the lawn in front of the Post Office, in case they came to check their mail. He wrote a postcard to Sarah at general delivery, telling her where he was. When he left there, he started walking over to the International Marketplace, to the guava juice stand. The sidewalk overflowed with sailors in tropical whites, pasty tourists in loud print shirts, hookers, Hare Krishna zombies, and locals trying to go about their business. He was almost to the marketplace when someone grabbed his elbow from behind. He turned, and saw Sarah, sunburned, nose peeling, dressed in a Muu Muu. They embraced, and people, gawking, had to walk around them.

"Now I know why Andrew insisted we leave twenty minutes early for the movie," she said. "I couldn't believe it was you when I saw you." She led him back down the street to where, double parked, Brother Andrew sat in the yellow Porsche. Chris squeezed into the back. Sarah strapped herself into the passenger seat, and they slowly drove off.

Brother Andrew wore a bright blue and yellow Hawaiian shirt, white cotton pants, and leather sandals. He was clean shaven, and his hair had been neatly trimmed.

"Your beard is looking very nice, Chris. You look just like Jesus."

"Was He at Cambridge with you, too?" Chris almost blurted out, but held his tongue. "How did you get the Porsche over here so fast? Telekinesis?"

"No," Brother Andrew laughed, "it just came off the boat today."

"You're going to a movie?"

"Not now. This calls for a celebration."

Brother Andrew went around the block and drove back up Kealakakua in the direction of Diamond Head. Sarah played nervously with the latch of her seat belt. They drove to a motel on a side street near the end of Waikiki, past the zoo, and went up to a second floor room. In the courtyard below, adults sat around drinking beer while kids splashed and shouted in the pool. The room was paneled in dark brown plywood paneling, with a fluorescent picture of Pele on the wall, ascending from a fiery volcano. There were two single beds, a table, a TV, and a kitchenette. Brother Andrew took a carton of passion fruit juice from the tiny refrigerator and poured three glasses. Motel glasses, short and stocky, with three ripples near the bottom so they won't slip through your fingers when you're drunk. They stood there, holding their glasses. Chris waited for Brother Andrew to propose a toast.

"Sarah and I were married last week, by a three-hundred-pound Captain in the Salvation Army."

Chris had never really looked at him before. He was short, five seven or eight. He had too much black hair on his arms. His face was slightly pitted, from acne probably, maybe small pox. His eyes were too close together. Sarah walked over to look down into the courtyard.

"Well," Chris said, holding up his glass, "to the lucky couple."

130

"There was about seven hundred in the Y.E.S. account," Andrew said. "I left it there for you. I trust you appreciated it."

"I gave it to Brother Pierre."

"Noble."

"I also wrote a letter to Sacramento saying I no longer had any affiliation with Y.E.S. in any capacity whatever."

The next day Chris brought over the film. They went out and rented a projector and screen, brought them back to the motel room, and watched the film three times. Then they went for a walk on the beach, and stood near a little kiddie pool, watching little kiddies play. Andrew and Sarah certainly didn't act like newlyweds; hardly touched each other at all. Maybe, he thought, it's out of politeness to me. Maybe Andrew hasn't learned to be demonstrative in public yet.

It was odd. It was like Chris was still hypnotized, intimidated by something. So much he wanted to say, to ask, to find out. Andrew maintained a cool façade, though, and Chris hardly had the will to try to break it. He finally was able to ask him "What are your plans?"

"We're leaving for India as soon as we sell the Porsche."

"Are you going to an ashram?"

"Good God, no! My grandfather is one of those pukka sahib regimental Colonels who stayed on after Independence to keep up the privileged life. He has a big house outside Simla. Say, why don't you two go for a walk while I go back to the room for a shower. It's so humid here."

Chris and Sarah continued their walk. "Will you stay in India?" Chris asked.

"No, we'll go to England."

"Lucky you. I wonder what Gerrie and all the others are doing?"

"I've thought about that a lot. I feel rotten about it. Andrew says it's working the way it was meant to. Gerrie and the rest learn something very important and we use the money to really get Y.E.S. to change the world."

131

"You believe that?"

"I have to. Oh, Chris." She stopped and put her head against his shoulder, and he held her in his arms. "You don't any more, do you? I wish you did; I feel so alone."

"You have Brother Andrew."

"Yes, but that's different. He . . . he . . . I told you once that if I were free to choose I would choose you, remember?"

"Yes, but I thought God was in our way, not Brother Andrew. Sarah, when did it start?"

"Oh, Chris, please don't ask me that!"

"Why did you come to sleep next to me that night at the training?"

"I thought I was never going to see you again. It was my way of saying goodbye."

She sat down on the sand, and began running it through her fingers. "There's a poem I read once, where Zeus turns into a swan and ravishes this woman, who conceives Helen of Troy. That's what it's like, Chris. It's scary. It's something so much more powerful than me. Don't laugh when I say this, but there's a stained glass window in our church in Woodside, Mary standing there, zapped by that dove from heaven, freaked, and wondering what the hell is going on...."

"I hope for your sake it works," he said, sitting down next to her on the sand.

"What are you going to do?"

"I'm going to look for a job here. I don't have enough money to get back home."

A week later Andrew and Sarah came by his room to invite him to supper. "Andrew has a surprise, I think," Sarah said.

They had almost finished eating when someone knocked on the door. Andrew jumped up to let in a big, short haired, uniformed navy officer holding a quart of beer in one hand and a cigarette in the other.

"Chris," Andrew said, "this is Lieutenant Johnson. He's a pilot on the Kitty Hawk."

Johnson put his cigarette in his mouth to shake hands. "Pleased t'meet ya," he said. "I got it," he added to Andrew. "Nine big ones." He reached in his pocket and removed a bundle of what turned out to be nine thousand dollars' worth of hundreds.

"Excellent," said Andrew. "Here are the keys and the pink slip."

The lieutenant left the beer bottle and a room full of smoke behind him. "Let me look," Sarah said. "I've never seen that much cash."

Andrew spread them out like a hand of cards. He plucked ten of them and handed them to Chris. "These are for you," he said.

"No."

"No, old chap? Sarah says you need it."

"I . . . I couldn't, I don't want it. Besides, I've got a job. I was going to tell you after dinner. At a missile base in the Marshall Islands, on Kwajalein. It's about twenty-five hundred miles west of here. I'm leaving July first. The pay is really good, much better than anything here."

"Take the money!"

"No, I don't need it. Send it to Gerrie."

A few days later he rode with them out to the airport, on the bus. Sarah cried. She hugged him one last time.

"Well, old chap," Andrew said, shaking his hand. "It's been a pleasure. I know it's been hard on you at times, but a little creative tension is good for all of us. Farewell!"

Chris watched them walk through the door and out to their plane. A little creative tension. Creative tension! How about a ton of it, pukka sahib? How about a million light years of the fucking stuff, you bloody hypocrite?

Ten

From the air, Chris thought, the atoll resembled a giant amoeba or a misshapen green eye floating in the vast blue sea. Closer to landing, it looked like a discarded necklace of trees. Only three of the islands displayed buildings; the airstrip was on the largest, next to a golf course. He left the plane and walked into a wall of sweating heat that not even his time in Honolulu had prepared him for. Waiting for him, holding the photo taken the week before in the World Services, Inc. office on Kapiolani Boulevard, was Don Bight, the Senior Clerk of the Marine Department. His skin was like brown rawhide, his frame stringy, as if the tropics had burned away all the fleshy parts. His black hair had been slicked down with some greasy lotion. He had bad teeth and eyes like a little snake. He acted a bit drunk.

Bight scrutinized Chris with immense pleasure. "Am I glad to see you," he said. "I've got work coming out of my ears. Let's go pick up your luggage."

"This is all I have," Chris said, lifting the satchel and sleeping bag upward slightly, as if testing their weight.

"You won't need that sleeping bag here," Bight laughed. They climbed into a battered pickup, and took the grand tour, mostly so Chris would know which areas were for the rocket scientists, officers, and their families, and off limits to menials like him. They drove then to the Marine Department offices, at the foot of a long dock extending out into the lagoon. Chris met McVee, who ran the department and piloted ships through the narrow, coral lined channel linking the lagoon and the sea. McVee carried a full ration of the aura of command that most ex-navy officers had picked up around the wardroom table. He was dressed for golf and had perfect teeth.

"I hope I won't have to look at that beard of yours much longer," McVee said.

Bight took him over to his barracks, showing him the cubicle he had been assigned. That night he found the library, in a cramped little room above the bowling alley. The rumble of careening balls and the knocking noise of pins came up through the floor. He wrote a letter to Bob and Nancy, promising to repay Bob as soon as possible. He read some of a book on Micronesia, then walked out to the ocean. He sat on the sand, with a warm breeze blowing in his face, and wondered if he could just keep going west forever.

Chris soon learned that Bight had lied about the workload. Mostly all he had to do was keep time cards for the boat crews. He designed a new, more complicated time card and rearranged all the files. He and Bight both had partitions around their desks. Chris read a lot, and when he heard someone coming tried to look busy. Bight always kept a pint of vodka hidden in his desk and typed long letters to his girlfriend in Seattle.

Supply ships arrived two or three times a week to maintain the Americans in appropriate style. When a ship docked, Chris received two hours pay at time and a half to help tie up the lines. If a ship came in at night or on weekends, it was an automatic four hours double time for what was usually about twenty minutes work. This, added to his regular salary of seven hundred dollars a month, would soon make him a rich man, especially since with free food and lodging, his expenses were almost nothing.

On the lowest rung of this socialist paradise were the Micronesians themselves. Many were Marshallese who had originally lived on Kwajalein or Bikini, and had been forcibly removed to Ebeye, the next island over from Kwaj. Others were from the Carolines and Marianas, lured by the prospect of paying jobs. They worked as maids, janitors, deck hands, dishwashers; a few were clerks or waiters. They could not live on Kwaj, nor use the stores, restaurants, bars, or hospital. A large ferry took them home to Ebeye each evening, and returned them for work early each morning.

One Saturday afternoon he rode the shuttle boat from Kwaj to Ebeye, just to explore. It looked like parts of Tijuana, or Olongapo in the Philippines. Dusty, no open space, streets lined with shacks knocked together from this or that; occasionally a real house. Kids everywhere. The little stores seemed to stock only canned soups, soda pop and Spam. All the women over thirty were either wretched toothpicks with brown teeth or else gone to considerable fat.

He bumped into Lejolan, the Marine Department janitor. About fifty, tall and lean but stooped, he had extremely long brown fingers and white palms. Lejolan carried a Polaroid camera on a strap around his neck, and took Chris' picture by the lagoon. Chris put the picture in his shirt pocket, and Lejolan dropped the backing paper on the ground.

Lejolan had very little English. "Watch?" Lejolan asked, pointing to Chris' unadorned wrist. "You have no watch?"

Chris shook his head. Lejolan reached into his pocket and took out a crumpled wad of bills. "Watch in PX," he said. "Eight dollar. You buy me?"

Chris took the money. They went back to Lejolan's house, a two room shack. Chris met his wife and seven children. Four wore ragged shirts and shorts, the youngest three were naked. Lejolan's wife expected another child soon.

"Speak English," Lejolan said proudly. "All speak English."

"Thank you, Lejolan, for letting me visit. I have to go, to catch the boat."

"I go with."

As they walked up the dusty street to the pier, they met a white woman. Lejolan greeted her. "Missy Anne, this Krees."

She looked about fifty-five, and wore a plain sleeveless white dress. She had her graying hair tucked up under a wide brimmed straw hat. She carried a small net bag stuffed with canned fruits and vegetables. Something about her bearing, her finely sculpted face, her sheer out of placeness on that wretched street suggested a heart of refinement and calm.

"I'm Anne Pennington," she said, in a soft Southern accent. "It's a pleasure to meet you." Then she shook Lejolan's hand, and spoke to him in Marshallese. He replied and she turned back to Chris and looked him over, as they say, from head to foot.

"Please come back to the clinic and have tea. Very few of the Americans ever bother to visit Ebeye."

Chris accepted, and said good-bye to Lejolan.

"You buy watch?"

"Yes, I'll remember the watch."

They walked down a block and over one to an ugly cinder brick building with a wooden sign reading "Friends Clinic." It had three rooms: an office/clinic, kitchen, and bed/sitting room. Anne heated water on a small electric stove. Somehow, she had managed to make the kitchen look homey.

"Did Lejolan give you money to buy him a watch?" she asked, as the tea brewed.

"Yes."

"He can't afford it, and he doesn't need it. And once you buy something for him from the PX, you'll be deluged with requests."

"Will you give this money back to him for me?"

"Yes, gladly."

They talked, and he found himself telling her everything about Brother Andrew, and the Children of Light, but not about Sarah.

"Lordy," she laughed. "Imagine, supposed adult men and women talking about the Children of this and that and Youth for such and such! They want to win the spiritual jackpot instead of going to church every week and banking the interest."

She talked about her home town. Westall Gap, North Carolina, nestled between the Blue Ridge and the Smokies. It wasn't really a town, didn't even have a post office, just a store

137

and a lot of families scattered around the hills. There was a community medical clinic, a small school, a summer camp, a Quaker Meeting and many good folks.

"You make it sound like the greatest place in the world. Why did you come here?"

"Well, the why is way too long of a story, but the where is easy. My husband was a conscientious objector, a medic in World War Two. He was killed on Kwajalein when the Americans took it from the Japanese. Have you ever seen photos of the island after that battle? There wasn't a single tree top left, just a forest of shredded palm stumps about four feet high."

They heard a knock on the door, and a stout Marshallese woman entered. She held a small baby, had a two year old girl clutching her skirt, and behind her, crying, stood a boy about five with a blood soaked dish towel wrapped around his hand. Anne quickly put on a white lab coat and washed her hands. She sat the boy on a chair, and unwrapped the towel. She and the mother spoke together in Marshallese for a moment while she was cleaning the wound.

As she was putting sutures in the boy's hand, she told Chris how the Marshallese weren't allowed to use the medical facilities on Kwajalein, and in emergencies had to be transported by helicopter to Majuro, the main Marshallese city on another atoll. She did her best with the minor problems, but found it hard to get supplies.

The little boy was crying from the pain of the sutures, and the little girl also began to cry. "Pick her up, won't you?" Anne asked. Chris did, and her crying stopped. Her deep brown eyes widened and looked intently at his face. A chubby little hand began to inspect his beard.

Later, after the mother and her children had gone, Anne made some more tea. When it was time for Chris to leave, to catch the last shuttle before supper, he promised he would come back. Anne opened her purse, and took out two dollars. "When you come back, can you bring some hydrogen peroxide? I'm almost out and can't get it right now on Ebeye."

138

"Yes, but put your money away. I'll pay for it."

He brought the peroxide the next weekend, and he brought a watch for Lejolan. Every two weeks or so Lejolan would ask for another one, and offer him eight dollars. He refused the money, but kept providing the watches. He never asked what Lejolan did with them.

He began going over every weekend. Anne held classes to teach adults to read and write Marshallese, and Chris started trying to teach some others to read and write English. He helped keep the place clean and learned to use the little sterilizing autoclave. He was on hand the weekend that Lejolan's wife, Monica, had twins.

He bought a cheap guitar at the PX, left it under his bed, and used the guitar case to smuggle aspirin, bandages, fruit juice, whatever he could buy that Anne needed. He worked out a system involving the schedules of the clerks in the various stores that made it less obvious he was buying so much. Even though he was paying for all of it himself, his savings kept growing.

Eventually, they caught him. A new security guard at the pier made him open the guitar case, and found vitamins, two sets of sheets, some cans of fruit juice, and a dozen fresh oranges that he had spirited out of the dining hall. McVee was pleased as punch and tried to fire him, but he only received probation. He could no longer risk carrying anything himself, but he and Anne worked out an arrangement where items would be brought over by one of the Micronesian housekeepers, who could easily hide them under the Muu Muu that covered her ample person.

At least once a weekend, Anne liked to walk up to the little beach on the top end of the island. The only bit of open ground left on Ebeye, it had a dozen or so palms and a view of the unspoiled island to the north. They would sit on a little wooden bench. More than once, she told him how she missed the change of seasons in Westall Gap, and lovingly described them, and the trees and flowers. She especially loved the rhododendrons, and how their leaves curled up when it was below freezing.

Late one Sunday afternoon, sitting on their little bench, she told him "A friend of mine in Westall Gap sent news. Our Quaker Meeting House needs a new caretaker. It doesn't pay anything, but there's a lovely little cottage with a view of the mountains, and you get asked out to supper a lot. I wrote back right away and told them not to hire anyone until they heard from me again. There's work around there, Chris. There's a summer camp, and people who make furniture. There's a print shop, and there's a school there, one of those alternative boarding schools. I have this feeling that you belong in Westall Gap."

"But I'm not a Quaker!"

"Well, you walk like a duck and talk like a duck. You're pretty close."

"Well, thank you, but I don't really want to go back to the States. If I leave here, I'll go to the Carolines, or the Philippines, or Indonesia. I want to get a job on a little cargo ship."

"How romantic. Maybe you'll die in a ditch somewhere, with one of the names of God on your lips. That would do the world a great deal of good, wouldn't it?"

He laughed. "You won't let me get away with anything, will you?"

"Let's go have some tea,"

He and Anne sat at her table drinking the tea. They heard a knock, and Lejolan entered, carrying his youngest son. Monica followed him carrying the six month old twin girls. All three children were sick, with high fevers. Lejolan and Monica were scared. Anne examined the children. She couldn't tell what they had, but it seemed very dangerous. Their fevers were too high, vital signs too weak. She sent Chris over to the police station to radio for the helicopter from Majuro. As he walked back, he noticed that a wind had risen, and saw dark, tattered clouds moving swiftly in.

Soon it began to rain, in sheets that the wind blew across the island almost parallel to the ground. Water blew in under Anne's door and formed a puddle on the floor. The thunder and lightning increased, and Lejolan went home to comfort his other children. The electricity went out. Anne lit candles, and they sat in the semi-darkness waiting for the storm to end, for the helicopter to arrive. Chris held one of the twins in his arms. She was hot, very hot, but not restless. Comatose, almost, as if in a drugged sleep. Quick, shallow breaths. He held her limp hand. From time to time Monica tried to nurse the twins, to no avail. Sarah put water in their mouths, using a little dropper. They held cool washcloths to the children's chests and foreheads. There was nothing else they could do.

The storm continued. Chris listened to the wind, the drumming of the rain on the roof. He heard a large piece of tin careen past on the street. He looked at the child in his arms and concentrated on what sounded like the calm assurances of Anne speaking to Monica in Marshallese. Then she turned to Chris. "Try holding a circle of light around yourself and the child."

It continued to rain and blow through the long night. At one point he thought the baby had stopped breathing, but then felt once more the little feeble attempts. If Someone from Headquarters, Someone with authority to negotiate, had approached him, offering to trade all future so-called bliss he might experience in this incarnation for the little girl's life, he would have made the trade. It would have been worth it, and it would have been the only thing he had left to give.

Near dawn, the wind began to fade, and the drumming of the rain ceased, and an hour or so later they heard the chirring sound of the helicopter as it approached the island.

Chris stayed on Ebeye all that day, doing what he could to help Anne and Lejolan. That evening, word arrived from Monica that all three children would be okay. He returned to Kwaj and fell into bed, exhausted.

141

The next morning he went into the Marine Department. Bight burst into that smirking grin he got whenever he was pleased with himself. "McVee wants you in his office."

McVee had the phone to his ear, setting up a golf date. He was all charm and smiles. He hung up and the smile disappeared. He looked up at Chris with the expression of a cat playing with a mouse. Chris had seen it often on junior officers. "Where the hell were you yesterday?"

"I was on Ebeye. Lejolan's babies were very sick."

"There's nothing in your contract says you get a day off if the janitor's got a little problem."

"One of his babies almost died!"

"You got no business over there. You ain't even got a woman over there, the way I hear it, unless you're popping that old nurse."

"You're sick, McVee."

"Yeah? Well, you're struck out, punk. Strike one is all that hair on your face. Strike two is you getting caught smuggling shit over to Ebeye. Strike three is unauthorized absence. Your year's contract is up in a month. We weren't going to renew it, but now you don't even have that. You're out of here, boy, on the next plane to Honolulu. We don't need gook lovers here."

"Can I quote you on that?"

"On what?"

"On the part about gook lovers. 'His supervisor listed cause of dismissal as . . .'"

"I never said that, boy. All that hair on your face must affect your hearing. Go talk to Bight about signing off."

The evening before they were going to put him on the weekly plane back to Honolulu, Chris went to one of the seaside bars. He took a table in a corner, where he could see the ocean and probably not be disturbed. He ordered an Irish Whiskey. He hadn't had a drink since before he had met Brother Andrew, and hadn't had an Irish Whiskey in many years. He started thinking about that summer a year or so

142

before he joined the Navy, right after he and his first true love had broken up, when he worked in the college library by day and sat in his little apartment by night, drinking Irish Whiskey and writing bad poetry. He ordered another one.

The day before, he had gone over to Ebeye to say goodbye to Anne. She had gotten kind of sappy about not getting sappy and not saying something like she loved him like a son. Then she got unsappy and lectured him. You're not cut out to be the Outcast of the Islands, she had said, you're too civilized. You really need to settle down and get sensible. He more or less promised her that he would go to the mountains of North Carolina and see about the caretaker job at the Quaker Meeting. He ordered another Irish Whiskey.

She was right, you know. He was too civilized to spend the rest of his life drifting from island to pillar to post. He would go visit Westall Gap, but even if he got that job, before he started it he would catch up on . . . on civilization. He had enough money. He'd go to Dublin, maybe, and drink Irish Whiskey and write bad poetry. Then up to Sligo, yes, to cast a cold eye on Yeats' grave, and chat him up about Leda and the Swan. Then over to bloody England, you buggers, to pay homage to Shelley's heart, in Mary's grave in Bournemouth, and on to Keats' house on Hampstead Heath, and maybe figure out where Sarah was, and make sure she was okay. Good old civilization. Chris always had been a bit of a fool, and as for turning sensible, well, not quite yet.

ANNIE'S COVE

One

The fourth grade is no good at all. Annie started it three weeks ago and hasn't learned anything different yet from third grade. The worst thing is that she has Mrs. Bark, who doesn't have any imagination in spite of how young she is. Annie had her for second grade and she was awful and now here she has her again. Why she had to switch Annie doesn't know.

The third grade was sort of okay because Miss Westall was nice and they learned cursive and fractions and times and divided by, which are handy sometimes. They grew beans and squash in little pots and learned where the continents are. Best of all they got to hatch baby chickens out of eggs right in class. Annie watched those eggs every chance she had and when they pecked themselves out she got to take hers home and it stayed alive because she put a little lamp inside its box and fed it on time. It was a girl and Annie named her Peeper and when she was big enough kept her outside and put her in the shed at night. Sometimes Peeper ate ants and Annie wondered what it must be like to have ants crawling around inside your stomach. Peeper was growing up fine until some animal went through a hole in the shed one night and ate her so all they found was one leg with a few feathers on it, which she and Lettie took up and buried by the magnolia tree. Annie cried some and Lettie cried a whole lot.

The second grade was awful, and that's when Annie began to hate school. She didn't learn a single thing new from first grade except a bunch of rules. Once they had to write a story about who they would like to come visit the school, and since she had been reading a picture book at home about King Arthur and the Round Table she asked Mrs. Bark how you spell Queen Guinevere, and Mrs. Bark said that lady had been

147

dead a long time and Annie had to choose President Reagan or somebody in gymnastics or something. When she told her Papa he said shit, he said Guinevere would still be alive six hundred years after Mrs. Bark was dead and forgotten, and he told her how to spell Guinevere, and she figured her Papa was right, not about spelling but about Mrs. Bark.

First grade was best because she learned how to read and she's been doing that ever since. She doesn't remember kindergarten very much but Lettie went just last year and she had fun because she got to draw pictures all the time.

When Annie gets on the school bus Robert Silver, like he always does, says there's Annie Fannie! Does anybody smell dago germs? The first time Robert called her a dago she asked her Papa that night what it meant and he said it was what some people called folks from Italy sometimes and she asked then why had Robert called *her* a dago? Her Papa said that back in the nineteen twenties the railroad got built over by Pineville and the people that built it were black people and folks from Italy. The families that had always lived here in this part of North Carolina had never had people like that around and didn't want them to stay around because they didn't know any better that they were just people like themselves only different, so they got in a mob with guns and sticks and rode donkeys up past Pineville and shot at those people and scared them all away. They already had mean names for the black people because they'd had them in the South so long being slaves and all until the Civil War, but those white people were the only ones they'd ever seen from somewhere else, so now any white person whose great grandpa wasn't born here they still call a dago because they're sort of stuck in a rut like happens to the station wagon sometimes when there is snow on the cove road.

Annie wishes she didn't have to go to school at all. She's wished that many times on Padma's candle. Padma has a wishing candle she took from the Buddha statue in the prayer barn, and a box of matches she got from a fancy restaurant in Asheville when Pam and Billy weren't looking. Annie asked her Mama if she could go to school at home and her Mama said no. Annie said but Padma gets to stay at home school and her Mama said right but that's because Padma couldn't learn to read in real school and Pam doesn't have to work. Besides, her Mama said, Padma doesn't learn nearly as many new things as you. Annie said if she stayed home she could teach Padma and Lettie to read and Pam could take care of them but her Mama said Pam didn't really even like to be bothered with Padma let alone Lettie and her, and Mama would like to stay home too but sometimes kids have to be like grownups and do things they don't want to. Annie doesn't think that's fair at all.

They were taking a break from putting the solar panels on the roof of the new building. Vance was looking at some specifications, Carol and Etienne were examining the vegetables in the garden, and Chris was sitting on his favorite bench, looking up at the mountains. Down here by Pam and Billy's house had always been the best place to view them. From here they seemed to rise up from the valley more precipitously than further up the cove.

He was looking at the Y-shaped scar up at the top of Sourwood Creek. One year before they had moved here, when they were still caretaking the Quaker Meeting House over in Westall Gap, it had rained seventeen inches in nine hours, and in the middle of the night that part of the mountain just gave way and crashed down the side. He'd gone up there a few years ago and there were still whole trees and huge boulders lying in big piles, and the scar was a smooth face of exposed rock. How long would it take for that scar to heal? Not in his lifetime, he knew.

Chris loved it here, in spite of the absurdity of Billy's venture, because he could mostly do what he wanted, compared to real work. And it was good for the girls to be as protected as they were from the world, but the world kept creeping in, and he feared he wasn't going to be able to protect them much longer. Around here, girls started getting pregnant at fifteen or sixteen, so eventually he would need to

149

take them someplace more sophisticated, which ironically would probably be safer for them. And that might be good for Sarah too. He had helped her escape a bad situation in London a year or so before they were married, and it had taken her a while after that to get her bearings. She had since then been becoming ever more comfortable with the real world, though Chris still had his doubts about the place. She kept studying how-to books and expanding her business skills, and seemed to thrive on it. Four generations of Old Baltimore Money were starting to show their effect, maybe, even though Sarah had grown up in California. California blindly liked to pretend that it was a classless society, especially back during the Sixties. East of the Mississippi, though, class still mattered, in spite of the fact that the plutocracy was capable of producing specimens like Billy.

But for now, Chris had these mountains, and his trembling love for Sarah and the girls, and Etienne's Gallic cynicism. The real world would just have to wait, especially since Vance said it was time to get back on the roof.

After they had finished putting the solar panels on the new building, Vance invited everybody out to dinner. First they all went up to Chris and Sarah's house to drink a beer, since you can't get beer in town. It was hard work up on that roof they said. They all sat on the porch and Annie and Lettie got lemonade. Purrseus was there too, washing his face with his paw like he always does. Everyone sat there for a while watching the sunlight glow through leaves, then they started in talking about Billy.

"Is he gonna be able to keep his head above water?" Vance asked.

"What head?" Etienne said.

"Billy never swims in the pond like the rest of us," Lettie said, and the grownups all laughed. Etienne said the rate Billy was going it would take him fifty years to break even, but he could afford it.

Then they went into town for supper. Billy and Pam had agreed to meet them there, at the Cowboy Corral, next door to the tire store where Annie and her Papa had bought the used tires for the station wagon once. Vance drove his truck because he lives in the motel in town where there's TV, but the rest of them piled into the station wagon.

Annie had never been to the Cowboy Corral before. You stand in line and look at all these pictures of meat and French fries and tell the lady what you want. Annie wanted Pepsi and Lettie wanted Mountain Dew. Everyone filled their plates up at the salad bar. The waitress was real friendly. She brought big pitchers of more soft drink and wondered if everyone was all right and she patted Annie on the head and said she had such beautiful long hair. Annie liked her a lot. Then the waitress brought Vance a big steak and she gave Pam a plate full of fried chicken. Billy's face started to look like he had a stomach ache.

"Did you order that?" he asked Pam.

"You were standing right next to me when I did. Padma, honey, you want some chicken?"

"I want two pieces, Mama." Annie was sitting next to her and watched her eat that chicken all up except for the bones. She sure wouldn't want to eat anything that had bones in it.

"These carrots taste like cardboard," her Mama said. "I'm sure glad we have our garden."

"So, Billy," Vance asked, "how much business you got lined up this fall?" His eyes were twinkling and he looked over at Pam and smiled at her. Her eyes were twinkling too. She was wearing one of those gypsy blouses so you could see the tops of her tanned breasts.

Billy coughed a little and wiped his napkin over his mouth. He didn't have much lined up yet, he said, but he was going up to New York next week to talk to a Swami from India about doing some retreats, and maybe he'd wind up pretty busy before Thanksgiving.

"Uh, when do you think you'll finish the hall?" he asked Vance.

151

"I can't rightly say." He'd finished his steak and he leaned back in his chair, putting his thumbs in his belt. "Depends on the electrician and the weather. I'll be away next week myself. I got to go down for a race in Charleston." He looked over at Pam. "Y'all ever do any sailing?"

"By the end of October, you think?" Billy asked. "You said mid-September when you started."

"Maybe. Maybe November."

"We sailed some with a friend in the Bahamas," Pam said, "four or five years ago. It was really fun."

"He wasn't any friend of mine," Billy said, and Pam looked at him and laughed.

"Mama," Padma said, "I want some dessert."

They all started in on dessert, then, except Billy. He said he was getting one of his migraines and went out to lie down in his car. Vance sat there drinking coffee and with his big shoulders and shiny blond hair Annie thought he looked like Aslan the lion who made Narnia. He sure smiles a lot, Vance does.

Padma wanted to ride home with Annie instead of with Billy and Pam. They sat in the way back. Lettie sat in the back seat between her Mama and Carol and cried some because she had spilled her ice cream, and then she fell asleep. Padma had her box of paper dolls and they played with them on the way home but then she started to feel bad and she threw up and got some on Annie's pant leg and some on her paper dolls but most on the rug of the way back. Annie's Papa stopped the car and cleaned it up with a towel. You could see little pieces of chicken in the throw up and they rode the rest of the way home with all the windows open and Lettie never woke up at all even after they got home so her Mama put her in her bed.

Annie thought it sure was nice of Vance to buy supper for all of them, especially at a place where the waitress was so friendly. She figured Vance must be pretty rich to be able to do it and asked her Mama if he was.

"Probably," she said.

"Is he as rich as Billy?"

152

"Probably not."

Annie said she didn't think so because he didn't seem to worry as much as Billy.

"That's because Vance is making money and Billy is spending it," her Papa said. He and Etienne were sitting on the sofa drinking more beers. Etienne laughed and said something in French, and her Papa laughed then too, but they wouldn't tell Annie what it meant.

After Billy left for New York, Padma and Pam went over to the beach at Edisto, South Carolina to get more tan. When Billy got home, he had some more migraines and went right to bed. When Padma got home, she told Annie that Billy said it was because the Swami was going to California instead of the Center since there were more people out there who wanted God than around here where there were too many Baptists. Vance came back from Charleston, too. He looked real happy, because he'd won his sailboat race, he said.

Two

Chris and Carol and Etienne were going to fix the bridge on the cove road, so Annie and Lettie ran down there past the ruined Old Home Place to warn the troll.

"Mr. Troll, Mr. Troll!" Lettie shouted, stomping on the rickety planks.

"Be quiet," Annie told her. She dropped a gravel rock down the knothole, like she usually does, to let him know it's her. "Mr. Troll, Papa's gonna come and tear this old bridge up. The boards will fall right on your head!"

"Run away, Mr. Troll," Lettie yelled, lying down on the bridge and sticking her head over the side, trying to see underneath. She leaned further and further down and Annie was afraid she would fall in the water. She grabbed the back of her tee-shirt and held on.

"Old Troll," Annie said, "you go hide somewhere, then you come back tomorrow night to a brand new home." She pulled Lettie's shirt, trying to get her standing up again.

"Annie, let me go!" Lettie screamed. "You're hurting my feelings!" Why she can't ever talk softly, Annie doesn't know.

Padma told them about the troll after they moved here to the cove. She'd lived here since she was born so she knew all about him. She said she had a little brother once but the troll ate him up. Etienne says the troll wears a cap with a Dixie flag on it, and chews tobacco and talks Southern. He spits in the creek, Etienne says, so you can't drink the water after it's been under the bridge. He has a white beard three feet long, and sea weed on his legs. Padma is afraid of him and never will walk over the bridge. She'll get a running start and do a ballet jump and only touch the bridge once to get across.

Lettie thinks Mr. Troll is a Baptist, because of something else Etienne said once. He said Baptists are Christians that've been thrown in a river and knocked their heads too hard on the bottom. Lettie gets things mixed up sometimes. Like germs. This year, the first morning on the school bus, Robert Silver said "Don't y'all go near Annie, she has germs. She's gonna rot up and die."

Annie asked her Mama if germs made you die, and she said some of them did, but not as many now days as used to.

"You get germs from cigarettes," Lettie said. "I saw a picture of it at the doctor."

"Robert Silver said if I got married my husband would catch my germs and die too."

"Don't worry about Robert, Annie," Sarah said. "He just sees stuff on TV and doesn't understand it, but he knows it makes grownups afraid. Next time Robert Silver says you have germs just tell him he doesn't know what the hell he's talking about."

Sarah was hoping to teach her daughters to stand up to men, and women too, for that matter. She herself had been conned and then bullied by her first husband, and then abandoned in London when he took up with the daughter of a lord and opened a New Age Institute in her ladyship's ancestral manor in Cornwall.

"Mama," Lettie asked then, "do you get germs from TV?"

"No, Lettie," Annie said, "you get germs from going to school."

Here is what school is like. They never do anything real. They make you draw a picture of a flower and label all the parts, but you don't use a flower, you use a big poster Mrs. Bark has. Annie would rather go over to the meadow and pick some different wildflowers and give them to Carol for her vase. All you do is paper stuff. It seems like no one even cares anything about the answer except if it's right or not. They make you study about feelings and personality and answer homework about them the same way you do about what's the capitals of North Carolina and Tennessee. Annie got one wrong answer because she marked letter B for feelings to answer where curiosity comes from but the answer was D for thinking. Her Papa saw it and got mad and said curiosity was thinking *and* feeling *and* experience and said maybe he'd call the teacher but he never did. In that test they had to answer what personality was, and traits, and feelings and needs, but Mrs. Bark never asked them how they felt or what they needed.

How Annie feels is she hopes the White Witch of Narnia makes it snow all winter so they have snow days and don't have to go to school. And what she needs, what she needs is for the boys to stop teasing her and the girls to be her friends. Lettie has lots of friends in school because she's pretty and likes to be nice. Annie doesn't have any friends in fourth grade and knows it's because she's too different. She always knows the answers and she's the only one who doesn't talk Southern. Her only friend is Padma, and Padma doesn't even go to school. All the girls in her class would just rather play with somebody else. They play silly games and pretend to be mamas or rock stars. Annie tried to play Mount Olympus once with Rose Etta, but she couldn't understand it.

What Annie really really feels is that she sure does wish the boys would just leave her alone. They tease her about everything, about things she can't help like when sometimes she pinches her neck with her fingers and her tongue sticks out a little bit. Or about the way she talks, because she doesn't talk Southern like them. They say she has germs just because her clothes are from the used store and a little dirty sometimes but she *likes* dirty clothes and that doesn't mean she has germs. She hates boys; they think they're so funny and that they know so much but she knows more about just almost everything than they do and that's one reason they don't like her. She especially hates Robert Silver because he's fat and he wears splotchy clothes like he's in the army and he always calls her Annie Fannie and sometimes he calls her Voodoo because she drew a picture of the Buddha once in class. He said the people at the Center are crazy hippies and dumb too because when they bought the cove from his Grandpa they paid too much and now his Grandpa is rich. She told her Papa she hopes Robert Silver takes his splotchy pants and goes in the army and gets shot, but her Papa said she shouldn't wish that even on somebody like Robert, but should wish he learns better ways.

The worst thing of all, though, is that people think Annie goes around stealing things. There's somebody that does, but it's not her. They take money or food or toys out of people's cubbies and no one can catch them. Robert Silver says Annie does it, and so do some other boys. Annie Stealer, they say on the playground. It's just not fair at all. Mrs. Bark even talked to her about it, and said it was no shame in being poor but did she know stealing wasn't right and Annie told her she wasn't poor at all, that she had more than a hundred dollars at the bank that her Grandma had sent her, and besides she wasn't any stealer and didn't take anything, but she bets Mrs. Bark still thinks she did. Maybe there's fairies at school who steal things, like the ones who take food from the Prayer Barn. Sometimes Annie thinks it might be Padma who does that and not fairies.

Annie's Mama and Papa have to work a lot to get money from Billy so they can put it in their checkbook. When people come for a retreat, her Papa and Carol and Etienne cook for them and wash the dishes and clean the dormitory and if it's cold keep all the fires big. At other times they have to fix everything that needs it and grow the garden and now that Vance is here building the Big Hall they help him, like when they put the solar panels on the roof. The rest of the days they go up behind the slave quarters where Billy has a hundred acres of trees and they cut firewood. Annie and Lettie go up there sometimes to help them and to look for fairy houses or play castle in the rhododendrons. There's an old oak stump with all these little mushrooms growing out of it, hundreds of them that look like half an umbrella. It's a fairy theater, and the fairies sit on the umbrellas while Annie and Lettie do plays for them.

There's lots of branches just lying on the ground up there because one day a big ice storm came and broke them. Billy owns a chain saw but Chris and Carol and Etienne won't use it. They cut up the wood with bow saws and two-handled ones, put it in a wheelbarrow and take it down to the slave quarters to put it in Etienne's truck. Many locust trees are dead but haven't fallen down yet and they cut those too. What Annie doesn't like is when they cut down living trees and kill the dryads. Carol says they only do that when the trees are too close together. Chris says it's good for the forest, like thinning carrots in the garden so those left behind can grow better, but still Annie doesn't like it when they kill dryads. There's one kind of tree that when Chris cuts down he calls the girls over to smell the wood, and it smells just like chewing gum.

It's hard work making firewood and they all get tired. After they cut enough for all the wood stoves, they take the rest into town and sell it and Chris puts his share in the checking account and Carol and Etienne put theirs in a coffee can in their cabin. Annie and Lettie like Carol and Etienne's cabin. In the winter it's always toasty warm because it's so small and they plugged up all the cracks. And in the summer it's cool because a big maple shades it in the afternoon. Etienne calls it the slave quarters but that's just a joke because Carol says there weren't hardly any slaves at all in Jackson County until the factories and TV came in. They're always baking bread or muffins or even cookies, and they give the girls some with big cups of juice from the apple trees down by the abandoned Old Home Place.

Padma says the slave quarters is haunted because some crazy dead old moonshiner used to live there, but Annie doesn't believe her because Carol is always playing her mandolin and singing about flying away to heaven or about Jesus. Ghosts couldn't stay in a place where people sing such pretty songs. Besides, Etienne says if any ghosts did come around he'd make a scary face like he sometimes does with all his bushy brown hair and beard and yell at them and scare them away because ghosts are almost as bad for privacy as telephones.

Etienne is from France over in Europe. He and Annie's Papa speak French when they don't want the girls to know something. Etienne speaks English pretty well, though, and Annie can understand him even better than some of the boys at school who talk Southern. Carol talks Southern, but not too much, because she's from Atlanta. Etienne says Carol has red hair, but it's not at all red. It's bright orange, the same as her freckles.

Etienne has a black leather scrapbook, about as big as the top of Annie's desk at school, and inside are pasted fancy face cards from decks of cards he bought when he lived back home in France. Those cards are from Vienna and Spain and London. Annie and Lettie love to look at the different queens and kings. Some of them are real people like Marie Antoinette and Richard the Lion Heart. Some are just made up and some are Indians and Arabs and people from Ancient Egypt, and there's one deck from the French Revolution that has no kings and queens, just workers and soldiers and a lady named Liberty wearing a toga. All the face cards in America are the boring old same, Etienne says. He loves his cards even though he hates real kings and queens. They should only be in scrap books, he says, along with all the presidents and generals and doctors and judges and teachers. Annie had a dream that Aslan from Narnia made all the trees in the cove come alive and they marched over and knocked down her whole school and nobody was hurt except Mrs. Bark who was run over and pressed total flat and they put her in Etienne's book but she was too big and her arms and legs and head stuck out so they had to fold her over two times to make her fit inside. Etienne says Annie and Lettie shouldn't have to go to school, and he's right of course.

One day earlier in the summer the three girls were helping Carol pick blackberries to make jam and sell it in town. Annie asked her why she and Etienne kept their money

159

in a coffee can instead of a checkbook like her Mama and Papa. Carol said it was because Etienne didn't have the right numbers here in America and there were lots of things he couldn't do. Well couldn't he use French numbers, Annie asked, and Carol said no, because in France he had gone to lots of meetings and thrown rocks at policemen and he'd helped burn down the stock market in Paris, but then his side lost and the winners wanted to put him in the army so he ran away to North Carolina.

"Does he need numbers for his truck?" Lettie asked.

"No, because we use my numbers for that."

"Why did he burn down the stock market?" Padma asked Carol.

"To make the bad people there go away," she said.

Lettie's hands and mouth were all purple from the blackberries, and so was her tee-shirt. "What *is* a stock market?" she asked.

Carol laughed. "Well I don't rightly know, Lettie, but Etienne says it's a place where rich people put all the money they've stolen from poor people so then they can steal it from each other."

Carol is a lot younger than Etienne but she lives with him because they love each other and he tickles her with his big beard. She's not as pretty as Annie's Mama but Etienne thinks she's beautiful, especially on the inside. Annie does too. They're not married like her Mama and Papa but her Mama says that doesn't matter. They met each other in Athens Georgia, which is not the same as Athens Greece near Mount Olympus, when Carol went to college and Etienne was sitting on the sidewalk selling the pretty necklaces and bracelets he makes out of little twigs. Carol says Silver Cove is a whole lot nicer than college.

Sometimes Chris and Etienne talk about college. They make beer in a big bucket, then they pour it in bottles in the closet and when they want to feel funny they put some in the refrigerator and drink it. Annie doesn't like the way it tastes but Lettie does, except for the sour part at the bottom. Sarah

160

and Carol drink some too but they don't tell stories like Etienne and Chris. They mostly sit quiet and whisper things to each other. Carol never talks much anyway. The kind of stories Chris and Etienne tell each other, Annie don't know if they're true or not. If they are, they both used to be just plain crazy.

They make jokes about Billy and Pam then too. Etienne calls Pam the Duchess, and says she pretends her blood is so blue it's a wonder she doesn't look like the picture of Krishna up at the slave quarters. He calls Vance the Sun King and he calls Billy the *Salaud,* which Annie figures is French for a Duke or something.

Etienne says Annie's Mama is the real boss of the cove. She works down in Billy's office that used to be a chicken house near the prayer barn. She talks on the phone and writes things on a computer and has a calculator and a book she keeps the numbers in. She has a big checkbook, too, that has different money in it than her own checkbook. These days she's always writing checks for Vance to build the Big Hall. It will be large enough for lots of people to pray in and dance around or do yoga or rub each other all over like they sometimes do. It has its roof on with the solar panels, but just plywood on the walls and floor and nothing inside but sawdust. The electrician still hasn't come to put the wiring inside it.

Vance built it mostly all by himself. Annie and Lettie and Padma got to put some nails in it. Vance came all the way from Chapel Hill because he knows about solar energy and most people around here don't. One day Annie and Lettie walked with Sarah up the hill back of the pond to the place where you can see the valley with the river in it and the big mountains on the other side.

"That's where Vance is from," Lettie said, pointing to the white church part way up a mountain. "Chapel Hill."

"No, Lettie," Sarah laughed. "Chapel Hill is a big city way down out of the mountains. That's just the country church, the one that rings the bell we hear on Sunday mornings."

161

They started walking back down toward the pond. "Why do they ring a bell?" Lettie asked.

"So folks will know to come and pray."

"How come we don't go there, then?"

"Because sometimes we go back to the Quaker Meeting," she said, "next to the house where you both were born and we had to move from because it wasn't big enough anymore. It's a long drive for us now, though, over an hour."

"I know," Lettie said.

They got back down to the pond and walked out on the dock. A dragon fly landed there, and they knelt down quietly to watch it. They could smell the alive smell of the water. The dragon fly's wings were shiny blue and green like a peacock feather and its whole body moved in and out when it breathed. Another one just like it flew down close by and they both went off playing tag. There were sparkles in the water, and the little water crawlers were going around zip zip this way, then that. On the water you could see the reflections of the bushes and the white clouds.

"See," Sarah said, "another reason we don't go to that church building is because church is everywhere, all the time. God made everything a miracle, and don't you girls ever forget that."

"If God made everything," Lettie asked, "then who made God?"

Sarah laughed a long time. "That's a question a lot of people have wondered about, Lettie. Ask your Papa."

That same night Chris took Annie and Lettie back to the pond to look for the water nymph and the monster. They stood on the dock and he shined the flashlight in the water. They could see some of the goldfish. One of them had a big round belly and Lettie thought it had swallowed a tennis ball or something, but Chris said it was probably going to have babies. Then he shined the light on the edge of the pond and they saw a bunch of tadpoles and two little salamanders and a crawdad. They never saw the monster or the water nymph.

Annie and Lettie got in an argument on the way home over who got to hold the flashlight, and Papa took it away from both of them.

"Papa," Lettie asked when they got home and were eating cereal, "there's one thing I really need to know. How come they make you hold your hands up before they shoot you?"

Chris looked kind of surprised. "Where ever did you learn about that?"

"At recess. Please, Papa, I really need to know."

"It's so you can't reach for your own gun, if you have one, and shoot back."

"Oh," Lettie said, and took another bite of her cereal.

Chris sat there for a minute and then he went outside and didn't come back until after Sarah put the girls to bed. Her Mama and Papa both scared Annie sometimes. Usually they were like winter when you can look across the road from their house and see the creek and the ground and all the bare trees on the hill with their praying branches, and even some of the far away mountains. Nothing could hide on that hill without you seeing it. Other times, though, her Mama and Papa were like summer when you can't even see the creek, just nothing but poplar leaves, and you can't walk down there because of the bushes and stickers and stuff. When her Mama or Papa are like that you can't tell what might happen. Annie is that way too, sometimes, or like the pond, so dark green and deep she doesn't know what's in her. Lettie, she's like the creek, pure clear, and she just chatters along.

Annie thinks Lettie is prettier than her. Lettie has blonde hair like their Grandma and her eyes are blue and she's lovely when she smiles except right now she's got this big empty space because her two top teeth came out. Annie's hair is brown like her Mama and Papa and she doesn't think she's pretty but her Papa says nonsense of course she is. As pretty as her Mama even, and some day he's going to have to buy a barbed wire fence just to keep the boys away from her, but she told him she'd rather have that fence right now because she doesn't like those mean boys at school one bit.

163

Annie is glad she and Lettie aren't boys. Her Papa says he's glad too because they probably won't have to be in a war. He was in a war. Sometimes he has nightmares and Annie figures that's what they're about. Sometimes she wakes up in the night and hears him kind of shouting from a nightmare. Sometimes her Papa and Mama have nightmares at the same time and Annie hears them both being noisy, but her Mama wasn't ever in a war so whatever it is she's yelling about Annie doesn't know.

Three

A bad thing happened. Purrseus ran away, or is lost, maybe, or some animal ate him up. Annie hopes not. She hopes he comes home. He's been gone two days now and Lettie cries all the time. Annie doesn't know why he had to leave. Yesterday morning he just wasn't here. He always waits on the porch and when he hears the first person wake up and walk around he scratches on the door and meows so he gets his food. He sleeps outside all night except in winter when it's really cold. He falls asleep with Annie or Lettie, of course, depending on whose turn it is, but before her Mama and Papa go to bed they come real quiet into the bedroom and take him out. Annie hopes he'll come home. She hopes he's just gone to find the three ladies with one eyeball to tell him where the Medusa is, and that Athena gave him the gleaming shield and stuff, then maybe someday he'll come back.

They have had him a whole year and a half, which is a lot more than that in kitty years. Mrs. Boone the egg lady said they could take him free and her Papa gave the Vet some firewood to get him his shots. Purrseus had to take a worm pill and have medicine to get the black stuff out of his ears. When he was older he had his balls cut off too and Annie didn't want that because she wanted him to be a Papa but the Vet told them that he would live five years longer if he had the operation. He said Purrseus would spray smelly pee in the house and get in fights and run away probably if he kept his balls, but now look, he's run away anyway, or maybe been killed. Annie hopes he comes home but if he does and is carrying a big bag she sure won't look in it because she doesn't want to be turned to stone.

165

She hopes he isn't dead, because being dead scares her. At first she didn't understand it, like when they'd find a dead bird or something and her Papa would say the Latin words after they buried it, but when she got older she realized it was forever, and she didn't like that. She suspects it's okay after you're dead, but it must hurt to die. Her Mama says she's just a kid and shouldn't worry about it, but she does, because she just doesn't know for sure. Lettie is named after Grandma Letitia, and Annie is named after a lady her Papa knew on an island once. She died because she was sick and nobody knew about it except her. When Grandma dies Lettie will be Letitia maybe and another Lettie will come along, and one day Annie will be Anne and another Annie might come along and maybe that's one way to get around it.

After school Annie and Lettie walked all the way up past the slave quarters asking the fairies if they'd seen Purrseus. Then they came back to the pond to ask the water nymph. They looked all around inside the Old Home Place, under the old junky stuff that her Papa and Etienne throw in there, and even went up the rickety staircase to the upstairs. Then they went down to the Prayer Barn to pray for him to come back. Padma was there with her wishing candle and after they prayed she wanted to play a game. Some games Annie doesn't like to play with Padma because Padma always has to say what the rules are. When Annie told her the first time about the water nymph Padma just took her right away and gave her a name and decided what color her hair was and whether she had a fish tail or not. But this time Padma just wanted to play paper dolls on her porch, so Annie and Lettie said okay. Pam was there too, reading a book with a fancy lady on the cover. She sits on that porch a lot and looks at the mountains and drinks coffee that she grinds up in a little machine.

Sarah and Carol are pretty, but Pam is the prettiest. She has long black hair and her eyes are like the sky at night with stars in it. She looks like the fine lady in the Mother Goose book Lettie has that used to be Annie's. The lady with rings on her fingers and bells on her toes. Pam always wears bracelets and necklaces and stuff. She doesn't have bells on her toes but she does have a little gold ring on one of them. Honest.

Her skin is even browner than the kids. In the summer she's at the pond more than anyone, and she skinny dips just like the rest, and puts shiny oil all over herself that smells like peaches. Sometimes Pam stays at the pond all day, just getting tan and reading books. She doesn't have to work because Billy is the boss. Sometimes she helps in the garden. She has a big straw hat that she wears then, and a pretty white dress that she bought in Europe. She takes a pair of scissors and cuts flowers and makes bouquets that she puts on top of her piano and the supper table. She picks tomatoes and lettuce and squash. My, what beautiful snow peas, she says. She talks Southern, but she lived in California once because that's where she married Billy and then they went off to India where she had the ring put on her toe.

Pam looks unhappy a lot, but Annie can't see why, though, because she's married to Billy and Billy owns the whole cove. Annie wishes she owned a whole cove. Billy owns it because he's rich. Etienne says Billy's Grandma came from England on the Mayflower and brought lots of money with her. He says that's the way most people get rich, from their Grandmas. Or sometimes they get rich from going to college and learning to cheat people. Her Papa and Etienne went to college but they just read old books and didn't learn how to cheat, so they're still poor.

The thing Annie doesn't understand is if Billy owns the whole cove how come he doesn't use it? He never goes up to the pond or walks around in the woods the way the rest of them do. He just stays in his office or in his house when he has one of his migraines, or he watches Vance build the Big Hall or he drives off to Asheville. He won't even walk out to the road to where the mailbox is, out where the school bus comes. Maybe he's afraid somebody will come along in a car and knock him down, like they used to knock down the

167

mailbox until he had Annie's Papa and Etienne put it in a little tower of bricks that looks like a chimney.

Billy thinks people around here don't like him because he's not a Baptist, but Annie's Papa says it's just kids in cars and they knock down everybody's mailbox, even Baptist ones. Billy must think Annie and Lettie don't like him either because he never smiles at them or plays games with them the way the other grownups do. He pays some attention to Padma, but he doesn't ever hug or kiss or tickle Pam or come up behind her and put his hands on her breasts the way her Papa does to her Mama. Padma says that sometimes Billy and Pam talk loud to each other and call each other names and sometimes Billy goes and sleeps on the couch, which must be hard because he's so tall. He's the tallest person in the whole cove even though he walks kind of stooped down a lot. Sometimes he makes Annie think of a big old dog. It's his eyes, probably.

Annie can't understand him when he talks. She can understand the words, of course. He talks Northern from when he grew up, but somehow he just talks on and on to her Mama or whoever and his words never go anywhere. Annie asked her Mama why, and she said Billy was only able to think or talk about himself and since he doesn't understand himself at all why naturally nothing that he says really means anything. Then her Papa said that Billy was just a spoiled kid who never had to grow up yet, and that's why he's not a very good boss and can't make the Center earn more money so they could have some more in their checkbook. Then her Mama said she didn't really care about that stuff because she and Papa had good food on the table and a nice rickety old house to live in and each other and two wonderful daughters, and all of them lived in the most beautiful cove in the world, no matter who owned it.

Four

On the last weekend of summer they went on a picnic. Annie doesn't see how they can call it summer vacation if you start school a whole month before the last weekend of summer. They rode over to the mountain, past where the man has all his roosters living alone in little round cages, looking out for Purrseus all the way, and they got out of the station wagon and walked up to the butt slide. The butt slide is neat. It's in a big creek and you sit down in the fast water holding on to this old root, then you let go and slide down a long smooth rock and the water makes you zoom really fast into a swimming hole. You don't skinny dip because a bathing suit keeps you from rubbing your butt too much on the rock.

The grownups mostly just slid down forwards sitting up, and Carol only did it once because she felt a little sick for some reason, but Annie and Lettie and Padma went down every way they could, on their backs and tummies, head first or feet first, arms at their sides, or straight out like a bird or an airplane. After a while they got goose bumps and their lips turned purple and Sarah made them come out of the water to wrap up in towels and sit in the sun. Then they had their picnic and went butt sliding again until time to go home.

Padma wanted to spend the night with them and that was okay. After supper they all made mazes for each other to do. Annie makes the best ones because she has a lot of practice putting the lines in order one after the other. Lettie and Padma make easy ones to figure out. Annie is pretty good with order. One thing that bothers her is the Narnia books are all out of order. They're numbered the way they were written, which is pretty silly because that's not the order they happen in, which is six one five two three four seven, and that's the order she keeps them in the box they go in. Why he didn't write them in the order they happened she's not sure.

At bed time they put their sleeping bags in the living room and Lettie cried some because Purrseus wasn't there, but Padma said the next day they'd go to the dock and light the wishing candle for the water nymph and Lettie could wish for him to come home. Annie said she thought Purrseus had probably killed the Medusa by now and maybe he was about to rescue Andromeda from the monster.

"You mean the monster in the pond?" Lettie asked, and Annie said maybe that *was* the monster Purrseus would have to fight. Then they all got in an argument over which one of them was Andromeda and Sarah had to come out and make them be quiet and pretty soon Lettie fell asleep, you could tell because of the way she breathes.

"Are you awake?" Padma whispered to Annie.

"Yes," she whispered back. And Padma made Annie tell her once more about when Lettie and she had gone over to the pond at night with their Papa to try to see the monster and the water nymph. You can't see the monster in the daytime because he crawls under the mud and goes to sleep, which is a good thing because otherwise he'd gobble you up when you went swimming. If you jumped in the pond at night he'd gobble you up total. He won't eat the water nymph though because he's in love with her, but she doesn't love him back. So he's sad like the Bog King of Egypt.

"I bet you didn't see them because you made too much noise and scared them away," Padma said.

"Lettie *was* being pretty loud."

"Let's try now! Are your Mama and Papa asleep?" Annie crawled real quiet down the hall and looked under their door and it was dark in there. She crawled back and got the flashlight from the shelf and they sneaked outside. They walked down the little path to the road. It was almost too dark to see. The locusts and peepers were loud as blazes.

"Should we turn on the flashlight?"

"No, and we can't talk no more at all so we don't scare them."

They walked up the road as quietly as they could, holding on to the waist of each other's nightgown. The wind felt warm on Annie's face but the gravel was cold on her feet. They found the break in the bushes and the wide spot where the dam is. They started to walk along on the wet grass of the dam to the dock when suddenly there was a light in front of them. Vance had lit his lighter and was holding it to a funny little pipe. They could see that he and Pam were sitting naked together on a blanket. Padma turned around and pushed Annie down to the ground. Then she pulled her up again and they started running back to the house. When they got back to Annie's yard, Padma grabbed her arm and they went in under the big pine tree and sat on the fairy table rock.

"What were Vance and your Mama doing? Were they skinny dipping?"

"Shut up. Just shut up. Don't you ever tell anybody what we saw. If you do, I'll never be your friend again."

They sat there for a while, and the noise of the locusts and peepers was like it was inside Annie's chest.

"I wish I had my wishing candle right this minute," Padma said.

"We could use the flashlight."

"No, somebody could find us. We have to pretend. What are you going to wish for?"

"For Purrseus to come home." Annie didn't ask what Padma's wish was, because she knew Padma never told. After a while they sneaked back into the house and got in their sleeping bags. Lettie was still breathing away. Annie was really worried. Padma knew a lot more about grownup things than Annie did, because when she and Pam went into Asheville for her ballet lessons, most of the time they went to the movies too. She told Annie about them once, but when Lettie wasn't around because Lettie wasn't old enough. In the movies, little kids get lost, banks get robbed, spies blow things up, and Mamas or Papas take off all their clothes and do things

171

with people called lovers that they're only supposed to do with each other. Maybe she and Padma would get in trouble for what they saw. Annie had funny dreams that night, and she bet Padma did too.

Five

On Monday after school Chris picked the girls up and drove into town. They put an advertisement in the paper saying Purrseus was lost. Then they went into the hardware store. Annie and Lettie don't go to town so much now that school has started. They like to go because they usually get some kind of treat, like when they go into the bank and the ladies there behind the bars give them a sucker. If they're going to the library they have to save the sucker until later because the library is right across the square from the bank. Once Lettie started licking hers on the way and they had to stand around looking at the flowers and the soldier statue until she was done.

Annie likes the library best of all because that's where the books are. She used to get books in the little kid's section like Lettie still does but mostly now she goes upstairs to the juvenile. She's not sure when she'll start on the grownup books, except some of the books that her Papa gives her like the *Prince and the Pauper* and the *Oliver Twist* book are almost grownup. She likes to be upstairs in the library because no one else ever seems to use it. She can listen to the librarians talk because there's just a railing up there and you can look down and see them. Her Mama says that living in the country is healthier than living in the city. It must be better than little towns, too, since what the librarians mostly talk about are sick people and operations that people had and people who died or how their wives are doing that were left behind.

The other thing the librarians always talk about is the weather. They don't seem ever to like it. It's always either too

173

hot or too cold or it's going to rain or it's not going to rain. She doesn't see why it should matter to them because they stay in the library all day anyway. Annie thinks every kind of weather is special, even rain. She likes to be up in her bed at night and hear it on the roof. Snow is best, because then she doesn't have to go to school.

Sometimes they go to the gas station with Etienne in his truck. He says things they don't understand, even in English, but they don't mind, because he usually buys them an IBC root beer. The men in the gas station talk about the weather too. There's always two or three of them who sit around inside on chairs and spit. They're kind of old and they usually have little gray whiskers on their face. One time Etienne told the girls that really those men sit in there and argue about people named Hegel and Kant, but whenever a stranger comes in they stop and slouch down in their chairs and touch their caps and one of them says "hit's likely to rain, I reckon."

After the library, the next best place in town is the grocery store. They always go first to the bakery section. They show the lady their cookie cards that they keep in the glove compartment of the station wagon and she gives them a free cookie. There's more food in that store than a person could ever eat. When Chris and Sarah have lots of money in their checkbook, Annie and Lettie can choose one new thing to buy, but sometimes they have to choose something different that's not so bad for them. The silliest thing in the store is the magazines at the check-out stand. They talk about a man who married a head of lettuce, or a pickup truck that cures sick people, or what movie stars are getting a divorce. There are pretty girls at the check-out who take your money and boys who put your food in the bags the wrong way so the fruit gets squished or something, and then they push your cart out to your car and put tobacco in their mouth. Sometimes in the store they see boys or girls who are in Annie's class at school and they usually say hello Annie because they're with their Mama and have to be nice and Annie says hello back to them but she knows they still don't like her.

174

Even Annie's parents don't have many friends in town or near the cove. There's Mrs. Boone's where they buy eggs from, who gave them Purrseus. And there's the old man who sharpens her Papa's saws. His name is Clarence and he lives in a house even more rickety than theirs. Chris takes Clarence some bread and some bottles of beer, and if it is summer some food from the garden. Clarence puts the saws upside down in a clamp and files them with a special tool while he and Chris drink a beer and talk about ships. Annie and Lettie like to visit him because he gives them things sometimes and sometimes there are puppies to play with. Clarence walks with a limp because the ship he was on was sunk by some men from Germany and he was in the water a long time and still isn't quite well. He always has little gray whiskers like the men in the gas station and his clothes smell funny sometimes but that's okay. He gave them a pretty plate once that he found in a dumpster. It says North Carolina and has dogwood flowers on it, and they have it on their bedroom wall.

Clarence grows tobacco and corn and has a field of Christmas trees he's going to sell when they're ready. One time when the puppies were crawling all over them, Lettie asked her Papa if she could have one, but he said they were too expensive because people raised them up for hunting. Lettie asked what does that mean and he said people teach some dogs to chase other animals up a tree so the people can shoot them. Lettie started to cry and asked why does Clarence sell them to people who raise them up like that and her Papa said it was because Clarence needed the money, the same way he sometimes has to cut down trees with dryads in them.

When they got home from town, Chris stopped at the Big Hall, and Annie and Lettie walked on up the cove road. When they were just past the Old Home Place they heard somebody call "Annie, Lettie, help!" from up across the meadow by the dormitory. It sounded like Etienne and they ran up that way.

"Here, Annie," he said, and they found him sitting on the ground. His face was all white and he was shaking. "You know how to telephone, don't you?"

"Sure."

"Then you run to your house and call anyone down at the Center. Tell them I fell off this roof and I think I broke my ankle. Do you know the number?"

"Yes."

"Then run, quick. Lettie, could you go with her and bring me back a towel?"

Lettie's eyes were as big as nickels. She nodded her head yes, and they dropped their lunch boxes and book bags and ran home as fast as they could. Annie phoned Sarah's office and she said she'd look for someone, and she would call her back right away. Meanwhile Lettie had gotten a big towel from the bathroom, and a pillow, and an apple and one of her teddy bears and a bottle of her Papa's beer. She started running up there carrying all that stuff, and tripped on the towel a couple of times. Sarah phoned back and said to go tell Etienne that her Papa would be right there.

Annie ran back up to the dormitory. Etienne was holding the beer bottle and Lettie's teddy bear in his lap. Annie told him about her Papa and a minute later he came driving up the road. Chris took one look at Etienne's swollen ankle and said they should go to the hospital.

"You know we can't do that," Etienne said.

"Then we'll go see a nurse I know who works in Westall Gap. I knew her Aunt too. She's okay, I'm pretty sure. Is Carol up at the slave quarters?"

"Leave her be. I don't want to worry her."

"On the way out we'll ask Sarah to bring her down to our house."

"And let's stop by your house on the way and get an opener for this beer."

The nurse said the ankle almost certainly wasn't broken, but the tendons had probably ripped and would take a month or so to heal. She taped it up and gave him some crutches, but under the circumstances, she said, she didn't see how he could get any painkillers.

"Brandy," Etienne said. "Brandy works." They had to go into Asheville for that, across two dry counties. Then they had to go to two liquor stores, since the first one only had Napoleon brandy, and Etienne refused to have anything to do with that fucking Napoleon.

Chris had called home from Westall Gap to tell them Etienne's ankle wasn't broken. Carol said the angels always watched out for people like him. She was pretty shaken up. Sarah told the girls to put themselves to bed, because she wanted to be with Carol. Lettie didn't even cry about Purrseus. She must have forgotten about him with all the excitement, and was soon asleep. Annie lay there thinking about angels and how they talk to that part of you that can't hear them. That got her to thinking about bugs, probably because she looks at bugs a lot and is pretty sure they can't hear her, so maybe they think she's an angel. Actually, she wonders *if* bugs think. There's these teensy little gray spiders on the porch sometimes that go jump without even moving their legs, and do they have time to think about it when they do it so quick? She can't imagine bugs just sit there all day without telling themselves stories or thinking about how pretty the sky is but maybe they just *feel* how pretty the sky is maybe they even feel God inside them in spite of they can't talk about it and are so tiny, and Annie was almost asleep when the porch light turned on and shone right in her window like it always does and her Mama and Carol walked out on the porch and Annie sat up and looked out the window and saw her Mama hug Carol and say "Don't worry about it tonight, love, there are still three or four weeks to decide," and that confused Annie a lot, because she thought that they'd decided that Etienne's ankle wasn't broken after all.

Six

The next morning Annie and Lettie walked down the cove as usual and got on the school bus when it drove up. Robert Silver, like he always did, said "there's Annie Fannie" and "does anybody smell dago germs?" She told him he didn't know what the hell he was talking about, like she does every morning now, and sometimes it shuts him up. At school they ate their free breakfast and then Annie went to class, which was boring as usual except they had show and tell. After lunch Mrs. Bark told Annie to get her lunch box from her cubbie and come with her to Mr. Ketchum's office. Mr. Ketchum is the Principal. Mostly he walks around the halls and smiles at you unless you're bad and then sometimes he hits you with a paddle he has in his desk.

"Annie," Mrs. Bark said, "would you open your lunch box for Mr. Ketchum please?"

Mrs. Bark took out the half eaten apple and looked under the used napkin. Lying there in the bottom was the little ceramic kitty that had been part of show and tell. "That," said Mrs. Bark, "belongs to Jodie Ann Shuford."

That was a mystery to Annie and she said she had no idea how it got there because she hadn't put it there. Mrs. Bark went out then and Mr. Ketchum talked pleasantly to her for a while saying why didn't she just tell him how it got there since she was such a good student and all, real cooperative usually, but she told him again honest she didn't know how it came to be there. He got a little angry then and told her to go sit in the room with Doris, the secretary, while he called her parents. Doris pretended she wasn't there and Annie sat a long time, then asked if she could get some water. Out by the water fountain was the board where they put your work sometimes

178

and she saw the things fourth grade had written about themselves. She read hers that talked about Lettie and Purrseus and the fairy theatre and how everyone skinny dipped in the pond, then she read some of the others and most of them said their best friends were so and so and none of them said Annie was their best friend, and she knew that already, but it made her sad to see it up there on the board that nobody liked her and now even Mr. Ketchum thought she stole things.

Then Chris arrived, and he put his arm around Annie and they went into Mr. Ketchum's office, and Mr. Ketchum told him straight out he thought she'd taken the ceramic kitty from Jodie Ann's book bag. Chris asked Annie if she had done it and she said no, and Chris said Annie wouldn't lie to him about that sort of thing. Mr. Ketchum wondered if she ever showed up at home with money or other little stuff that Chris didn't know where it came from and Chris said no, and Mr. Ketchum said that maybe she could hide it away somewhere.

Annie could tell that her Papa was becoming angry. He asked how they knew the kitty was in the lunch box in the first place. Mr. Ketchum said a student had seen Annie put it in there and told Mrs. Bark. Chris asked what student and Mr. Ketchum didn't want to say. Chris said everybody had a right to face their accuser, and if Mr. Ketchum wasn't willing to do that then he thought the accuser had put it there because Annie's word had always been a good one, so she should just go on back to class. Mr. Ketchum said he was sorry, but he had to protect people's property at the school, and Annie couldn't come back unless she confessed. Chris said that was bullshit, and he was so convinced Annie wasn't a thief that he was going to get a lawyer so she could go back to school.

"You don't have to do that, Papa," Annie said, because she knew Chris and Etienne didn't like lawyers at all, and because she'd just figured out what they were saying, that since Mr. Ketchum thought she was a thief she didn't have to go to school. If she'd known that all along, maybe she would have stolen something back in the second grade.

179

"Before you get a lawyer," Mr. Ketchum said, "you ought to have a real long talk with that little girl. I seen a lot of parents before who were mighty surprised when the truth was finally drug out."

"Let's go, Annie," Chris said, and they went on home. She didn't quite know how she felt because she was glad she didn't have to go to school but she didn't want everybody to think she stole things. She was afraid they'd start saying mean things to Lettie now too. On the way home Chris told her he believed she was telling the truth but he'd ask her just one more time before he started to go raise hell with a lawyer he knew from Quaker Meeting who he thought might give him some free advice. Annie told him honest, she didn't do it but she thought maybe it would be the best thing if she and Lettie just stayed home anyway so they could get a *proper* education. Chris laughed and said maybe she was right but it was really best if they stayed in school because he and Mama had to be busy working and besides maybe the folks around here could learn that we were really just like them, or just like they used to be back when they were poor too and before there was all this talk about the Devil.

When they got to the Center, Annie stayed in the car while Chris went in to talk to Sarah. Padma was at her ballet lesson in Asheville. Vance and Carol were working on putting windows in the Big Hall. Then Chris drove Annie up the cove road all the way to the slave quarters. Etienne was sitting in bed with all his jewelry makings scattered around, holding a glass of brandy, with the bottle on the bedside table. Chris told him about Annie being sent out of school and then they spoke French a while. Etienne asked Annie since his foot was hurt so much maybe she'd like to come up to his house in the days and help him out some making necklaces and soup until her Papa got her back in school. Annie said that was just fine and maybe he could teach her some French too so she could understand what he and her Papa talked about sometimes. Etienne laughed and said *mais oui* but some of the words he and her Papa used he couldn't teach her because somebody might put him in jail. He said all the necklaces she helped him make he'd give her some money for if he sold them at the Christmas fairs.

After Chris left, Etienne showed Annie what kinds of twigs to go collect so he could make the beads from them and she went out in the woods and got a big bunch and then Etienne showed her how to cut the string just the right length on the yard stick while he cut the twigs into pieces and sanded the ends and drilled a tiny hole through the center of them.

On the wall opposite where the picture of Krishna was, there was a poster of a big bulldog. Someone had drawn a Salvador Dali moustache on it. "What's that picture?"

"That's the University of Georgia Bulldog."

"That's where you met Carol."

"Yes," Etienne said, and took a big sip of brandy. "Do you know where your Mama and Papa met?"

"Papa said they were in some kind of club together in California."

"That's right. They wore funny uniforms and put up tables in front of grocery stores to sell cookies."

"That's the Girl Scouts who do that!"

"Yes, but their club did it first, until somebody stole all their cookies. Then the girl scouts moved in on their territory. Your Papa's had a hard life, Annie."

"I know. He was in a war."

"Worse than that, Annie. Do you know who Shelley and Keats are?"

"Papa reads us poems from them, sometimes."

"Well, your Papa went all the way to England once because he wanted to say a prayer to Mister Shelley's heart. He thought the heart was buried with Shelley's wife, but then he found out it was buried with Shelley's son, and that disappointed him a lot. Even more, though, he found out that a college professor somewhere proved that Shelley's heart would have burned up in the funeral fire because hearts are hollow, and that it was certainly Shelley's liver that his wife had kept flat in a book for so many years! Your Papa hasn't been right in the head since."

"You mean that made him turn crazy?"

"No, it made him turn sane."

Annie was still cutting string when Carol and Lettie showed up. It was becoming cold outside and their cheeks were red and Carol's long hair lay around her shoulders thick and soft and shining orange, and she was smiling and Lettie was chattering like always and Annie could see the life in them more than usual, which happens sometimes to make you remember how God made everything, people and bugs and flowers all having something extra special inside them.

Carol gave Etienne a big kiss and she gave Annie and Lettie each a peanut butter cookie, then the girls walked on home. Lettie asked her how come she'd left school early like the bus driver told her and Annie explained they thought she was a stealer, which she wasn't, but they didn't want her to come back. Lettie understood right away and said it wasn't fair at all if she still had to go to school and when they got home she started crying and got real mad at her Mama and Papa when they said she had to keep going, and she cried more and kicked and fell asleep on the sofa.

"Thank God," Sarah said.

After supper Annie started reading the *Oliver Twist* book that Chris had bought her at the used book store in Asheville. Folks didn't treat Oliver Twist fair either. Not at all. Her bad stuff was not nearly as bad as his, but still it was pretty bad lately. Purrseus being lost, and seeing Pam and Vance skinny dipping that maybe would get her in trouble, and Etienne being hurt and her being called a stealer which she still couldn't decide about how bad it was since she got to stay home. What she didn't know, when Sarah made her stop reading and go to bed, was on that very night there would happen the biggest thing of all.

182

Seven

When Annie woke up the next morning, Chris and Sarah were sitting at the table drinking tea. Chris' clothes had black on them and you could see where he'd washed it off his face and hands. He looked real tired.

"How come you're all dirty, Papa?" she asked him, and he told her that the Big Hall had burned up in the middle of the night, all the way down to the ground. He had been helping the fire people after Billy phoned him, but there wasn't much they could do at all because it had already mostly burned down before the fire people got there. Were the solar panels and the windows all burned up too, she asked, and he said everything, because the fire was so hot.

When Lettie woke up, Sarah said she didn't have to go to school that day after all. They ate some breakfast and got dressed and walked down the cove after Sarah went up first to tell Carol and Etienne. The Big Hall was burned up, all right. There were piles of black stuff with smoke coming out of some of them, and puddles of dirty water and a twisty metal mass that used to be the solar panels. The roof was gone but some timbers stood up like big burned match sticks.

Vance was sitting on the hood of his pickup truck. Pam was standing next to him, holding one of her fancy coffee mugs. Billy and Padma were sitting up on their porch, looking at the mess. Then Etienne's truck came down the road with Carol driving it and Etienne sitting on a blanket in the back with his hurt leg stuck straight out. Carol pulled the truck up close to Vance's.

"Mother of God!"

"Yep, Frenchy," said Vance. "All my tools too."

Carol started to cry and put her head down on the steering wheel. Sarah got in beside her and hugged her, and Carol put her head on her shoulder and cried some more.

Etienne asked how it had happened, and Pam said they weren't sure, that it was probably an accident, but that Billy was convinced the Baptists had done it. Annie and Lettie went up to see Padma. Billy didn't even say hello to them and they went inside to Padma's bedroom and played paper dolls with her.

Later that day the fire department people came back to poke around, They were there a long time. They asked if anybody smoked cigarettes, or if Vance had been using torches or anything and said they couldn't tell yet what had happened. The next day some inspectors came all the way out from Asheville and looked it over the same as the first bunch, and they couldn't figure it out either. Billy was convinced it was deliberate, but they called it Origin Unknown. Billy said of course they were in cahoots, and if it was a Baptist church burned down he bet they would have found the reason.

That fire caused so much stuff to go on that Annie almost forgot about school and being called a stealer. Sarah was making phone calls all the time, and a lady came from the newspaper, and a fat man named Mr. Snotgrass or something like that came from the insurance people. He didn't have any hair on the top of his head, and he had a big book he kept notes in and he talked to her Mama and Billy a lot and he wanted to talk to Vance too, but Vance had already gone back to Chapel Hill. It seemed like there was always some meeting where everybody went and people were talking about secret things because they would get quiet about it whenever Annie or Lettie or Padma were around.

Lettie only got to stay home two days and then she had to go back to school. That didn't please her one bit and Sarah walked her down the cove to make sure she got on the bus. Annie helped Etienne out some, and then she went for a walk in the woods to gather twigs. The ferns were starting to turn red and curl up. There were some coral mushrooms like her

184

Papa had showed her, mostly pink but some yellow and one even purple. She would tell Papa about them so he could come pick them. There were some bright red fairy tables and little teensy fairy umbrellas and some pink mushrooms so big she could have sat on them except they would break. Many of the mushrooms looked old and kind of rotten. It was sad. Lots of the leaves on the trees, too, were starting to get holes in them or little brown spots, and she thought about in spring when those same leaves were tiny and fresh green and new and she decided the next time she wished on Padma's candle she'd wish that nothing ever died.

She started to think about how she would home school. She could read books from the library and could learn things from her Mama and Papa and Carol, and Etienne could teach her to speak French and even write it. Carol is a good teacher. She'd taught her things like the leaves of the white oaks have round edges like a white cloud and the leaves of the red oaks are pointy like red flames. And Annie had taught herself that the maple has leaves like the Canada flag and the poplar has ones like a pretty dress for paper dolls and the locust has little leaves that look like necklaces of teardrops. She knew what poison ivy looks like too.

It was hot in the afternoon and she went down to the pond. The pond could be her school if she stayed home. She had learned a lot there. Sometimes she sits still and quiet just like the two snakes, the one that sleeps on the stump and the other one on the old fencepost that leans out over the water. That's how she discovered once that everything moves. Trees move, all the time, even if it's just a tiny bit. The hillside over past the pond is never really still. The water moves, and the little water crawlers move on the water, looking for dead baby crickets and things. The shadows of the trees move. They start at the edge of the pond in the afternoon and move toward the tethered raft and the dock. The shadows get to the raft first and when the sun goes further down they cover the dock. Etienne says the sun doesn't really go down. It's big and far away and the earth turns up real fast and it just looks like the

185

sun goes down. Annie is sure he's right because he showed her pictures of the planets and stars and galaxies in a big book he has. Lettie thinks that to a spider, the cove must be about as big as the whole universe, but Annie told her no, spiders aren't that much smaller than people.

Annie took off her clothes and swam out to the tethered raft. Lying there on her back with her eyes closed, the wood was warm, and it smelled nice. Her skin was cold but after a few minutes she began to feel toasty. A drop of water ran down her side and at first she thought it was a bug. She was glad people said she was a stealer.

Then what do you know. That evening just when they had started cooking supper a car drove up the cove and stopped at the house and Mr. Ketchum got out. They stopped cooking and everyone sat on the porch.

"That's quite a fire you had down there," Mr. Ketchum said. "I heard all about it from one of the boys on the truck."

But he didn't come because of the fire. He came because he wanted to apologize to Chris, as he'd found out Annie wasn't a thief. One of the mothers had phoned him to say Robert Silver had bragged to her son that he'd gotten Annie in trouble by putting the kitty in her lunch box. And now they'd found out that Robert Silver had been the thief all along. Mr. Ketchum apologized to Annie too. Grownups make mistakes sometimes, he said. He wouldn't say who had told on Robert, but he thought the boy liked Annie but was afraid to be her friend because of the other kids.

"Maybe he'll be your friend now, Annie," Mr. Ketchum said.

"I bet he won't."

Mr. Ketchum allowed as how he had believed Robert was telling the truth to Mrs. Bark because his wife was a cousin to Robert's Papa, and he thought he knew Robert pretty well. But when the other boy told, Robert had fessed up after his Papa had knocked him around some.

"Will he be kicked out of school?" Chris asked.

186

"Only for a few days, because he's fessed up and his Papa is going to take him to the County Health so they can help him not be a thief."

Mr. Ketchum asked if they knew that Silver Cove used to belong to Robert's family and Chris said yes and Mr. Ketchum said Robert's Papa never forgave Robert's Grandpa for selling out the family place and probably that rubbed off on Robert and made him want to be mean to Annie because he was jealous. Mr. Ketchum's wife used to visit here when she was a little girl, he said, and swam in that very same pond down there.

"Perhaps she'd like to come for a visit or a picnic, or even to swim," Chris said.

"Why that's quite friendly of you."

"Would you like a beer?"

"Well, I don't care if I do!"

They heard somebody else driving up the cove, and it was Clarence in his old truck. He parked next to Mr. Ketchum's shiny car and got out.

"Why, how you doing, Clarence?" Mr. Ketchum asked.

"Can't complain, Harry. How's your Pa?"

"He's doing poorly, I'm afraid."

"What y'all doing up here?"

"Just school business, Clarence."

Chris gave Clarence a beer too, and Clarence asked him over to the truck to talk privately. They looked in the back a bit, then Chris called Sarah over and Annie and Lettie wanted to go but Chris said they couldn't. Sarah looked in the back too, and then they talked some more. They returned to the porch and told Annie and Lettie to go get in the back of the truck to see something Clarence had. They climbed in and there was just a dirty old sack. Clarence took a drink of his beer.

"Got something for you little sweethearts if'n you want it."

Lettie said sure but Annie asked what it was and then the sack moved and Clarence picked up one end and out rolled a little brown puppy with giant black eyes. Lettie started to jump up and down and holler but that scared the puppy so Annie made her stop. After a minute they managed to get the puppy so it was half on Annie's lap and half on Lettie's.

"What's her name?" Annie asked.

"Well, in the first place, it's a him. And I don't rightly know his name, 'cause he come from the dumpsters."

"You mean somebody threw her away?" Lettie asked.

"You could say that. Some folks can't bear to shoot the critters so they leave them tied up at the dumpster. Like I say, it's a him."

"What should we call her, Annie?"

"Let's call him Dumpster for now, but we'll find a Greek name for him soon." They took him out of the truck and Annie ran and got some of Purrseus' dry cat food and Dumpster gobbled it all up.

"Girls," Mr. Ketchum said, "that's a mighty fine dog you've got there."

"Did you thank Clarence?" Sarah asked, so they did.

Dumpster wasn't acting scared at all, so they went up to show him to Carol and Etienne and he followed them all the way like he knew he was theirs now. Etienne was sitting in bed making necklaces, and drinking his brandy for his foot. Carol was playing on her mandolin.

"Look at his feet," Etienne said. "He'll be big when he's grown up. Do you girls know what the melting pot is? That's something your teachers will tell you happens in this country, people from all over becoming one big family. Really, it's mostly only true for dogs and cats, and your puppy wins the prize for having so many different grandparents that the only breed you can call him is American!"

Carol started to sing a song about a dog called Old Blue. "Let's call her Old Blue," Lettie said.

"No," Annie said, "because he's not old and he's not blue, and anyway, that's not Greek."

"I like the name Old Blue," Lettie said as they were walking home. When they got back, Mr. Ketchum and

188

Clarence had gone, and supper was ready. Chris and Sarah wouldn't let the puppy come into the house, and Lettie cried. Chris said he'd fix up a nice little place in the shed.

The next morning was Saturday. Both girls woke up early and went out to the shed to see the puppy. He had a torn blanket to lie on and some dishes for food and water and a little piece of fire wood he was chewing. He was happy to see them. Lettie hoped nothing would come into the shed and eat him up like it had Peeper, and Annie told her he was too big for that.

At breakfast Lettie was still calling him Old Blue. "But I *want* her name to be Old Blue," she would say. Annie had given up trying to tell her he wasn't a she, and so had her parents.

"No," Annie kept saying, "I want his name to be Greek."

"I know what," Sarah said, "here's a good compromise." She took a piece of paper and wrote in big letters C-E-R-U-L-E-A-N. "It's a pretty kind of blue paint that I use when I have the time to paint. It's not Greek, but it's ancient Roman, which is almost as good."

Lettie liked that name. "I'll call her Old Cerulean," she said.

After breakfast they went running in the meadow with Cerulean, and Lettie pretended to be a wolf cub like in the elf books, then they decided to go down to Padma's so she could meet him. When they came to the troll bridge he started barking like crazy and running from one side to the other, looking down in the creek and whining.

"You hush, girl," Lettie told him. "You'll wake up Mr. Troll and he'll gobble you." They kept going and he followed them until he ran over and started sniffing all around where the Big Hall had burned up. At Padma's, Billy was talking on the telephone, but he stopped and told them Padma wasn't home. Then he said he was talking to their Mama right then and she said for them to head back up to the house because they were going into Asheville.

Cerulean had to go back into the shed so he wouldn't get lost while they were gone. In Asheville, Sarah got out of the station wagon to go talk to a lawyer about the fire. Then Chris took them to the shoe store and bought them both a new pair of warm winter boots. Then they walked over to the red brick Catholic Church and Chris sat there with his eyes closed for a bit while Annie and Lettie looked at the statues and the stained glass windows. Annie liked the white doves with haloes best of all. After that they went down to the art museum in the basement of the Civic Center, where the girls crawled on the rhinoceros statue, which is what it was there for, until Sarah showed up. She and Chris sat for a while talking, and then they went to Ike's for lunch.

Ike was there as usual, behind where you pay. He took them to a table and gave them menus and Annie and Lettie some crackers the way he always does, sort of sliding the packet across the table to them like it was a secret message or something. Ike has gray hair and a big stomach and a painting of himself on the wall dressed in a Turkish costume, because he's from Turkey, which is right near Greece, and is where the Trojan War was. There are nice photos on the walls of a beach and a mountain and a tower and a castle. After lunch Chris and Sarah ordered coffee, and Ike brought over two suckers, one grape and one cherry.

"I like Ike," Lettie said, which for some reason made her Papa laugh.

"Girls," Sarah said, "I've got some news for you. Pam and Padma have gone to Chapel Hill. They'll be back in a few days, but then they're going to move there for good."

"Are they going to live with Vance?" Annie asked. Sarah looked surprised, and then said yes, they probably would.

"Mama, why are they going to live with Vance?" Lettie asked.

"Because Pam has decided she likes Vance better than Billy."

"You mean Billy isn't going too? Then isn't he going to be Padma's Papa anymore? Is Vance going to be her Papa?"

190

"Billy will still be her Papa, Lettie, she just won't live with him all the time."

"But I don't want Padma to go away!" Lettie shouted, and she started to cry, so Chris took her outside while Sarah and Annie paid and Ike wished them a lovely day. When they got outside, Lettie wanted the cherry sucker and Annie did too, but Lettie was still feeling so bad that Annie said she could have it, and took the grape one.

Eight

On Sunday, Chris and Carol and even Sarah started in to work on the Big Hall. Chris knocked down what he could with a crowbar. They made a pile of pieces of wood that hadn't been burned, which weren't very many. Some pieces were part burned and part good and they sawed off the burned part and put the good wood on the pile. On a second pile they put all the wood that was mostly burned up. They sorted out all of Vance's tools that they could find and threw a lot of them on a third junk pile, but Chris saved some for himself and they put some in Etienne's truck, and Carol and the girls drove it up to the slave quarters so Etienne could limp out and see if he wanted any, which he did, and the rest went back on the junk pile.

Vance didn't want any of the tools because the insurance company was going to buy him all new ones. Clarence showed up and put some stuff from the junk pile into the back of his truck. He patted Cerulean who rolled over and peed on himself.

"You remember that galax we talked about, Clarence?" Chris asked. Clarence nodded. "Well, anytime you want to come pick it now, it's all right."

"Maybe if these girls of yours will help me, they'd earn them some money off of it." One time Chris had showed the girls what galax was, and said some people picked it to sell to flower shops. That seemed silly to Annie, since it wasn't a flower, just a leaf. But if she got money for picking it, that would be okay. She wouldn't pick all of it, though, so it could grow back.

Monday morning they had to go to school, and left Cerulean in the shed so he wouldn't follow them down to the

192

bus. Robert Silver wasn't on the bus, which felt good to Annie because nobody teased her, but then at recess Timmy Hensley called her a tattle tale, and said she'd told on Robert Silver and got him in big trouble and she was just a damn old tattle tale. Annie wondered if maybe it was Timmy had told on Robert and just then Lou Ann and Rose Etta came running right into her like it was an accident and knocked her down and laughed and said don't them heathens have rules against tattling, and Annie said you don't know what the hell you're talking about and started to cry, which she only did at school once before, when she got her knee all bloody. She'd have to ask her Mama or Papa what a heathen was.

The whole rest of that school day was just as bad. When they got off the bus, Annie wanted to be alone and talked Lettie into going up and helping Etienne make necklaces. She told her he'd probably give her *two* cookies and Lettie ran on up there. Annie went into the garden and counted the red tomatoes that were left. The leaves of everything were shriveled up because there had been a frost. She looked for a bit at the mess that used to be the Big Hall, then she looked around and didn't see anybody, so she went into the prayer barn. She didn't know why Billy didn't want kids in the prayer barn except maybe he thought they'd go in the kitchen part and take food. Annie wouldn't do that, though, because everyone knows now that she isn't a thief. She piled a bunch of the round pillows together and lay down on her tummy and looked at the Buddha statue that's in there that Etienne says Billy paid too much money for. It's so heavy that nobody could steal it though. That Buddha looks real happy.

Annie sat there listening to acorns go plunk on the tin roof from the big oak tree, and thought about what her Mama had told her about the Buddha. He was a real rich prince but then he saw some sick and old and dead people and figured that would happen to him so he went away and only ate rice in a bowl that poor people would give him and he sat under a tree for seven years until he got lightened and saw that the secret of life is not to want any desires, and that made him able to see the way things really are, which we can't normally do. Annie gets lightened sometimes when she can see a special light in everything like the day Carol and Lettie had red cheeks, but she hasn't learned not to want any desires yet, and that's what she wanted to think about. Because she really didn't want to go to school any more at all. It wasn't what she *wanted* that made her unhappy, it was what she didn't want, school and the bad things that happened there. She didn't want to be bored all the time, and teased and knocked down. She didn't desire that at all.

So she asked the Buddha to help her think, and after a while she figured it out. She was unhappy because of the way things were at school and if she just kept thinking about that she'd stay unhappy. But if instead she thought about what she could do to stop being unhappy, then she'd be thinking about something besides being unhappy and she wouldn't be so unhappy. Mr. Ketchum was pretty nice most of the time, except when he thought she was a stealer. Maybe she could go talk to him, like Jesus did to the grownups in the stained glass window in Asheville. She could tell Mr. Ketchum how bored she was and that people thought she was a tattle tale when she wasn't. Maybe he could help her. Maybe if she told Mrs. Bark she would rather read *Oliver Twist* than do a whole page of commas and periods in the right place when she already knows where they go anyway, Mrs. Bark might let her. She started having all sorts of good ideas. She could work at it more ways than one, even. At the same time she could try to convince her Mama and Papa to let her stay home. She could teach Lettie stuff and Carol and Etienne could be her teachers too and maybe she could talk to Billy because it seemed like he was a big reason she had to go to school because he didn't want her and Lettie to bother her Mama and Papa while they were working, even though he didn't pay them hardly enough money anyway. She figured she could go in right then and talk to Billy if he was in his office and not at home with one of his migraines.

194

She put the pillows back in rows so nobody would be mad. Then she went up and touched the Buddha on his knee. The stone was cold. Actually the whole room was cold and she realized she was shivering some, but Buddha looked like he felt warm and peaceful inside, and she thanked him for helping her think it out even though he might not totally agree with what she came up with because she still wanted some stuff but she just wanted true stuff not any bad stuff that hurts people.

Annie ran over to Sarah and Billy's office and went in the door. She didn't think Sarah was there until she walked in a few steps and saw her through the other doorway where Billy's desk was. She was in there rubbing Billy's shoulders, him sitting with his head on the desk. That scared Annie a lot. She didn't want her Mama to go away with Billy.

Billy was talking like he always does. "I didn't want any of it anyway," he said, in a whiny voice. "It was always Pam's trip. I didn't want to go to India and live with all that garbage and when she got pregnant and it was finally too much for her there too I didn't want to come to this crappy place. She thought she'd be the Lady of the Manor and when the locals just ignored her she thought we should start the Center and people would just flock here, and we'd become big shots. She should have just started a stud farm. That's all she really wanted."

Sarah was still rubbing his back and neck and shoulders. "She's going to get one hell of a surprise this time, though," he said. "I guarantee you that. I'm calling the shots now."

Sarah got a funny kind of smile on her face, and shook her head. She looked over and saw Annie through the doorway. "Hello, pumpkin," she said, "where's Lettie?"

"She's up at the slave quarters," Annie said, and then remembered she wasn't supposed to call it that around Billy. "Mama, can I go pick a tomato?"

"Sure."

"Mama?"

"Yes?"

"Will you come with me?"

Sarah looked at the clock on Billy's wall and said yes, she would. She told Billy she'd see him in the morning. In the garden, Annie picked the biggest red tomato she could find and ate it while they walked up the cove to home. She had just arrived home when Padma called. Padma had just arrived home also and said Annie should meet her at the troll bridge. She let Cerulean out of the shed and went on back down the cove road. Padma was already waiting for her when she got to the bridge.

"You stay on that side," Padma said, like Annie was an audience or something. She had a big rock in her hand and was tying a piece of yellow string around it. Cerulean went over and sniffed her legs and then sniffed around the bridge.

"Is that your dog?"

"Yes, his name is Cerulean."

"Where'd you get him?"

"Clarence gave him to me and Lettie. He found him at a dumpster. He was free."

"That's the ugliest dog I've ever seen."

"No he's not," Annie protested. "He's just got big feet. He'll be beautiful when he grows up, like the ugly duckling."

"Me and Pam are going away. We're going to live with Vance in Chapel Hill."

"I know. Mama told me."

"How did she know?"

Annie just shrugged her shoulders. Cerulean was down in the creek drinking the water. Padma finished tying her knots around the rock. "After the Big Hall burned down," she said, "I figured Vance would go away, but I sure didn't think he'd take me and my mom."

"Maybe you could come live with me and Lettie."

"No, I'm going to Chapel Hill. My mom said she'd be damned if she'd leave anything behind for my dad. I'm going to go to this special fancy school and Vance is going to give me a computer and I'm going to take ballet and tap dance and eat ice cream cones afterwards. And Vance is going to take us to Disney World and Italy."

Padma walked over the bridge toward Annie. One of the planks went rattle and she remembered the troll and gave a little scream and started running on ahead. Annie caught up, and ran with her past the Old Home Place. When they got to the pond, they went out to the end of the dock.

"You close your eyes, Annie, and put your hands over them."

She did, and could smell the tomato smell on her hands. Cerulean was standing back on the dam, whining, afraid to come out to them. Annie couldn't tell what Padma was doing, but she heard the sound of her matches rattling in the little box. She just couldn't help herself so she gave a little peek. Padma was tying the match box and her candle to the rock with that yellow string. Annie closed her eyes again and wondered about that. She wondered if Padma was tired of her wishes not coming true, but finally figured that since she was going away she was just going to give the candle and matches to the monster and water nymph once and for all. She thought about asking if she could have them for herself, but she knew Padma would know she had peeked if she did, and then she heard a plop sound in the water and it was too late.

"You can open your eyes now," Padma said. Annie opened them and saw a wide circle of ripples going out to the edges of the pond, rocking the yellow leaves on the water like boats in a little ocean.

"What did you do?"

"Nothing," Padma said, and then they went up to Annie's house. Lettie was back from the slave quarters. They played elf, and as usual Lettie wanted to be the wolf cub.

When Pam called up for Padma to come home, Annie and Lettie walked her as far as the troll bridge. She got there before they did, because she ran past the Old Home Place but they didn't. She was standing on her side of the bridge, waiting for them. Cerulean ran across and jumped up on her, and she kicked him away harder than she needed to.

"It's starting to rain," she said, and turned and ran down the road.

You can't feel the rain too much when you're on that part of the road where the trees provide cover, but when they got up to where the meadow starts, where the Old Home Place is, they were getting pretty wet.

"Come on, Lettie," Annie said, and they ran over the rickety little foot bridge up to the old porch. The rain was sounding like little rocks were falling on the rusty tin porch roof. There was no front door, so Cerulean went inside to sniff around and was excited about everything he could smell. Sometimes Annie wishes she could smell as much as a dog, except when she smells something bad that makes you want to hold your breath.

Lettie's hair was all wet and had a tiny leaf in it, and she had a big drop of water on the tip of her nose. Annie wiped off the drop. "She can smell more than we can," Lettie said.

"How come you always call him a her, Lettie? He's a he. You know that, don't you?"

Lettie had a sad look on her face. "Yes, but I'm trying to change him into a her so he won't get his balls cut off."

"They don't do that to dogs, Lettie, only to cats."

"Really?"

"Really. Dogs don't run away even if they've got their balls."

"How do you know they don't? Did Papa tell you?"

"No, Mama did, because I asked her."

"Well how come nobody told me? That hurts my feelings! How come I *always* have to be younger than you?" She started to cry, and Annie put an arm around her.

"Because I was born first, Lettie. But listen, the older we get the less hard it will be. Look at Mama and Papa. He's a whole seven years older than her but there's lots she can do better than him. Pretty soon you'll be able to read as good as me and that should make you happy, and you'll know as many things as me and when we get older the boys will like you more popular than me because you're prettier."

"It's too hard, Annie. It's too hard when everybody is bigger than you."

"Cerulean isn't bigger than you." Lettie was shivering, so Annie zipped up her jacket for her. Cerulean came back out on the porch. Annie picked him up. He was wet but warm, and squirmy, and he started to lick her face.

"Here," she said, and gave him to Lettie. "You're such a good wolf cub you can be his Mama. You tell him we're not going to cut his balls off, because I forgot to."

Cerulean was licking Lettie's face and getting mud on her jacket, but she was giggling and happy. Annie was glad she was happy because she gets so sad sometimes, sadder than Annie ever does, and sometimes for no good reason, even, like just because she's a little kid. She hugged Lettie, and Cerulean squirmed around between them and started licking Annie's face again too. Then he tried licking both of them at the same time, and they got to laughing so hard they all fell down. Cerulean was climbing all over Lettie now, and she kept laughing. The rain had almost stopped. Annie stood up and helped Lettie up and said let's go home, and they did, and they held each other's hand all the way, and when they got home Sarah made them get in a hot bath and they had so much fun they splashed too much water on the floor, but Sarah didn't get mad at them.

Chris built a fire in the wood stove, the first one they had had since spring. Lettie wrapped up in her blankie and fell asleep on the sofa before supper was ready, because supper was late. Afterwards, Annie sat in her parents' bed and read some more of *Oliver Twist*. Sarah talked on the phone to Billy a long time, but Annie couldn't hear what she was saying. Chris picked her up and carried her into her own bed, and then carried sleeping beauty Lettie into hers. He kissed Annie goodnight and a little later Sarah came in to kiss her too. It was raining hard again, but their roof wasn't tin so it didn't sound like rocks, it sounded like a big wind in the woods.

"Mama," Annie asked her, "you're not going to go live with Billy, are you?"

"Heavens no, sweets, what makes you think that?"

"Well, you were rubbing his back and stuff in the office and I thought maybe he was your lover."

"Annie, I was just trying to make him feel better. He's been having a real hard time lately, what with the fire and Pam leaving and all. You don't need to worry about that sort of thing. Papa is my lover."

"Papa's not your lover! He's your husband!"

Sarah laughed at that one. "Sometimes they're the same person, pumpkin."

"But most of the time they're not, aren't they?"

"A lot of the time they're not. Now you go to sleep. We can talk tomorrow if you want."

Annie felt a lot better then, because she really loved her Papa and she didn't love Billy at all, and wouldn't want to have to go live with him somewhere, though he'd be better than if she had to go live with somebody like Robert Silver's Papa who knocked him around until he fessed up. She'd heard that some kids' Mamas and Papas *like* to knock them around and do it sort of for fun until the police come and take them away, and she thinks that's awful. Her Papa doesn't even like to yell at them but he has to sometimes. Maybe she should try to pay more attention like he says. Please God help Lettie grow up happy instead of sad and me too. Please Buddha .... And then she remembered about all the things the Buddha helped her to figure out what to do.

"Mama," she yelled, and after a minute Sarah came in. "Mama, can I stay home from school tomorrow?"

"As a matter of fact, you can. You and Lettie are going to stay home with Papa and Padma. Pam and Billy and I are going back into Asheville."

"Mama, why didn't you tell me that already?"

"I just forgot, sweets. I've got a lot on my mind."

"Mama, you should pay more attention, like Papa says."

"I wish I could. Now go to sleep, love."

200

Nine

Something woke Annie up in the middle of the night, and after a minute she knew what it was. She climbed down from bed and ran to the front door and put on the porch light. Purrseus was standing there on the porch all wet. He just kept meowing even after she'd opened the door. She picked him up and he didn't weigh anything at all, and she got a towel, and wrapped him up. He smelled real bad and hissed and jumped down when she tried to dry his back. She ran into her parents' room and woke them up.

"Purrseus came home!" They both got up and went out into the living room.

Purrseus was lying on the sofa, wrapped up in the towel, and he was purring. Chris opened up the towel and looked him over. "Poor kitty, he's been bit or something on the base of his tail and it's infected. We'll have to take him to the Vet tomorrow."

"We should feed him," Sarah said, and when she went over and opened the door under the sink where his food was, he jumped down and ran over there meowing.

"I'll go wake Lettie up." Annie said.

"Oh please don't. She can wait until tomorrow to find out."

"That's not fair, Mama. Purrseus is home! We can't treat Lettie like a little baby all her life!"

"Not so loud, Annie," Chris said.

But just then Lettie ran out of the bedroom and yelled "Purrseus!" Chris told her to be real careful of the wound, and she sat on the floor holding him straddled over her legs as he ate his food. All of a sudden she began to cry. "Papa, we don't have to take Cerulean back to the dumpster now, do we?"

Chris laughed. "No, he's part of our family now. We'll just have to teach him not to mess with cats."

Annie and Lettie both wanted to have Purrseus in bed, but Chris said no, that he should stay on the sofa and towel because he was hurt, and besides he smelled bad.

In the morning they put him in a cardboard box and went to town, to the Vet. They were in Etienne's truck because Sarah had the station wagon, and it was crowded because Padma was with them and they were all in the front seat with the box on their laps because Chris wouldn't let them ride in the back all the way to town in case they fell out. The Vet said how glad he was that Purrseus had come back to live with them. He sat him up on the big leather table and Annie kept him calm while the Vet gave him a shot, which didn't seem to hurt him at all. He took Purrseus' temperature too and asked Annie if she knew what her temperature was supposed to be and she said ninety-eight point six and he said right, and told her a kitty's normal temperature is one hundred and one. He asked her what grade she was in and she said fourth, and he said he bet she got good grades and she said a ninety-four was the lowest she ever had on a report card, and he said he could tell she was real smart and he bet she'd make somebody out of herself some day and she said she already had.

When Sarah came home from Asheville, she'd been to the fancy market and had all kinds of things. She had those long skinny baguettes that Lettie and Etienne like so much, cheeses, and some little chocolates for everybody, and some passion fruit juice that Annie and Lettie had never had before, and two bottles of champagne she put in the freezer to get cold quickly. She gave Padma a chocolate and told her that her Mama was home so she should run on down because the two of them were going to go into Asheville again right away. Annie and Lettie didn't want to go with her to the troll bridge because they were playing Vet and had to take care of Purrseus.

202

Chris went up to tell Etienne and Carol about the champagne, and Etienne walked all the way down to the house on his crutches, and said he would throw them away real soon. They opened up a bottle of champagne and started in on it, except Carol said she only wanted one little glass. Annie and Lettie had their passion fruit juice, and began playing mazes while the grownups talked. Etienne held up his glass and said a toast, everyone, to Lawyers and Silver Cove, and they all clinked their glasses and cups.

"I thought you didn't like lawyers," Annie said.

Then Chris and Etienne started in drawing mazes too, and they got some scotch tape and taped more pieces of paper together and opened the other bottle of champagne and pretty soon almost the whole floor was covered with a big taped together maze everyone had made and the only problem was none of them could figure it out.

Sarah cut up some more baguettes and put cheese on the pieces and they started in eating again. Then she said "Come over here and sit still, girls, I have a lot to tell you." She said that she and Papa and Etienne and Carol were going to buy Silver Cove from Billy and Pam, but they weren't really going to own it because the lawyers were going to make a piece of paper called a land trust that said it was really God who owned the land, like the Cherokees had said in the first place, and even if they all moved away one day, no one could ever sell it again or cut the trees all down or build big buildings on it.

"Do we have enough money in our checkbook to buy the cove?" Annie asked.

"No, but we just have to pay a little money every month to Pam, and I'll be in charge of the Center now and we can probably have enough for all of us and still pay Pam. And if we ever don't have the money, Grandma Letitia has signed a piece of paper saying she'll pay Pam for that month."

"We'll work too," Annie said, "making the twig necklaces and picking galax, and give you some of our money. But why don't we give the money to Billy?"

203

Etienne laughed. "Because Pam's lawyer is a lot smarter than Billy!"

Sarah told them the insurance was going to pay to build the Big Hall again, and that would be a good help for the Center, and she was going to work harder than Billy had and get more people to come and she'd even let the Baptists come if she could talk them into it.

"I bet you can," Annie said.

There's more, too, Sarah said. Billy was going away also, to Chapel Hill to be near Padma and try to get her back. And they were going to move down to Padma's house, and the girls could each have their own bedroom if they wanted it, and there would be a room they all could paint pictures in.

"Can we have a piano too, Mama?" Lettie asked.

"Maybe. And Carol and Etienne are going to move into our house here so they'll have more room." She looked over at Carol. Carol smiled and said she and Etienne were going to have a new baby, and she hoped Annie and Lettie could help take care of it sometimes.

"If it's a girl I will," Lettie said.

Then Etienne said that the lawyer who did the land trust was going to get him his numbers for free, and that he and Carol were maybe going to get married, and then they'd have a party and after that he might become an American like the rest of the harlequins in the cove.

"Can me and Cerulean live in the slave quarters?" Lettie asked.

"No," Chris said. "You still need to live down with us. Mama is going to rent out the slave quarters like a motel room for people who want someplace quiet to meditate."

"Then can me and Cerulean stay there when it's empty?"

"Sure, sometimes, when you're older." Sarah said. "But listen girls. There's one more thing, and I think you'll like it. We're going to try an experiment. We're going to take you out of school and see how you get along. Annie, you'll have to be Lettie's teacher, to make sure she learns to read and write and do math, and you'll have to study too, and not just sit around

204

reading Narnia books every day. You'll both have to let us do our work too."

"You mean we get to home school?" Lettie asked.

"Yes."

"YAAYYY!" Lettie screamed, and she started running around and twirling and messing up the mazes, and Annie started jumping up and down on the sofa, and Chris made them put on their shoes and coats to go outside.

Sarah was zipping up Lettie's coat when Etienne said "I'll tell you a secret, girls. If you home school, your Mama and Papa won't have to get up so early."

"Shhh!" Chris and Sarah both said.

Outside, the wind felt cold on Annie's cheeks. It was blowing so hard that hundreds of leaves were coming off the trees, thousands of them, maybe, flying down the cove above the tree tops. A noisy flock of crows flew up there too, all black against the gray clouds.

"Caw, Caw," Lettie shouted, running around and swinging her arms up and down. Cerulean came out from under the porch, barking and wagging his tail.

Annie looked at the hillsides with their swaying trees all green and brown and red and orange and yellow, and at the crows and the leaves and the speeding clouds.

"Let's go down and tell Mr. Troll," Lettie said.

"And the Buddha," Annie said.

They ran down the cove road flapping their wings, and Annie thought she just might up and fly.